CHRISTOPHER
COOL

X Marks the Spy

In the thrilling city of Paris, TEEN's crack espionage agent Chris Cool undertakes a baffling and dangerous mission: to ferret out a revolutionary new secret weapon which could change the balance of power in the cold war. His contact is an unknown spy identified only by a cunningly concealed X mark. When three men turn up with X marks, Chris is faced with the grim challenge of correctly identifying the right contact.

Chris and his Apache fellow agent, Geronimo Johnson, follow a clue that leads to the Riviera resort town of St. Tropez and discover that they themselves have become the quarry in a blood-chilling game of hide-and-seek with the deadly agents of TOAD.

For all mystery-spy fans, here is a suspense thriller packed with pulse-pounding excitement that never lets up till the final paragraph.

TEEN
Agent

CHRISTOPHER COOL

X Marks the Spy
Mission: Moonfire
Department of Danger
Ace of Shadows

TEEN
Agent | CHRISTOPHER COOL

X
Marks
the Spy

by JACK LANCER

GROSSET & DUNLAP
PUBLISHERS   NEW YORK

Contents

X
Marks
the Spy

1 · The Fun House

SPRING HAD COME to Kingston University. The April breeze ruffling the ivy on the mellow red bricks of the bell tower was growing warmer.

So was the watch on Chris Cool's wrist. The lean, blond sophomore felt the metal case burning his skin as he strolled across the campus with his Apache roommate, Geronimo Johnson.

"Hot flash from Control," Chris murmured.

"Let's go, *choonday*," said Geronimo.

They headed for a bulletlike Jaguar on the parking lot near the dormitory. Chris slid behind the wheel and the copper-skinned Indian youth took the bucket seat beside him.

The 4.2 liter engine purred like a well-fed pussycat, then broke into a full-throated jungle

1

roar as the gleaming black Jag shot down the driveway into Madison Circle. Beyond the arched campus gateway, the car rolled swiftly through the quiet colonial streets of Kingston, drowsing in the late-afternoon sunshine.

"Humph!" Professor Adlai Rowbotham frowned primly as they tooled past. "Cool again! Most brilliant student I've ever had, yet there he goes—off to New York for another night on the town. Young idiot would rather moon away his time in some bleating discothèque, I suppose!"

On the open highway Chris reached under the dash and drew out the radiotelephone.

"Kingston One to Q."

There was a moment's pause before the voice of TEEN Control responded in his usual fake British accent, "This is a Green Most Urgent."

"Understood."

"Ever heard of a place called Funland?"

"Affirmative. It's an amusement park on the New Jersey Palisades."

"Go there. Look for a man in a dark suit, bushy black mustache, red-blue striped tie."

"And when I find him—?"

"Identify yourself by rubbing your left eye, then yawn. Once you make contact, proceed with extreme caution. Hear what he has to say."

"Is he one of ours, sir?"

"No idea. Chap just phoned Cloak and Dagger in New York"—(this was Q's pet name for the

Central Intelligence Agency)—"wanted someone to meet him at this Funland place. Said he had vital information on a CIA man named Anson, Ivor Anson, who's missing in France."

"How come they handed us the job, sir?"

"The fellow sounded terrified. Said he was being followed and whoever met him must use the utmost caution. Cloak and Dagger felt a TEEN agent might stand less chance of being spotted. . . . Now listen. This could turn into rather a sticky wicket, so watch your step."

"Understood." Chris shoved the radiotelephone back into its receptacle.

"*Naha'ashla?*" Geronimo inquired. "What's the pitch?"

Chris found himself slipping naturally into the Apache tongue as he relayed Q's orders. The boys often conversed in the curious-sounding language—a code that no enemy eavesdropper or lip reader could possibly crack.

Both had volunteered for their dangerous role as secret agents. Geronimo, coming from the greatest race of guerrilla fighters in history, with the blood of Apache war chiefs in his veins, had been naturally attracted to the stealthy, deadly business of cold-war espionage.

Chris had a stronger reason. His father—Dr. Jonathan Cool, America's foremost brain in high-energy physics—had disappeared during a scientific conference in Europe, two years ago.

Convinced he had been kidnapped by enemy agents, Chris vowed to find him.

Only seventeen at the time, Chris had applied for CIA training, with little hope of being accepted. To his surprise, he had been tapped at once—not for the CIA, but for an organization he had never heard of, called TEEN. This hush-hush corps of bright young students had been specially developed by Intelligence on the theory that its members would be less open to suspicion than older agents. The name stood for Top-secret Educational Espionage Network.

Already a genius at languages, Chris could pass as a native in several different tongues. After rigorous training in electronics, photography, cryptography, flying, scuba diving, karate and aikido, he had been enrolled as a freshman at Kingston, an Ivy League university, where he found himself rooming with a fellow TEEN agent, Geronimo Johnson.

The Jaguar raced north on the Garden State Parkway and turned off onto Route 46 leading east to the Hudson River. Funland sprawled along one side of the sign-cluttered New Jersey highway. An enormous Ferris wheel and looping roller coaster tracks loomed above other amusement rides.

Chris slid the Jag into an open space at one end of the parking lot. A leather-jacketed motorcyclist on a Honda stared enviously at the sleek car. His lip curled to wisecrack at Geronimo's long black hair. But the Indian's cold stare made him kick his engine to life and zoom off.

Daylight was fading as the sun sank behind a low-lying cloud bank. Neon signs were flashing on in Funland. Chris and Geronimo bought tickets and went in through the turnstile.

"What's the drill, *choonday?*"

"Circulate around the midway, I guess, and keep our eyes peeled."

They moved slowly through the early Friday evening throng. Gaudy signs proclaimed the attractions.

FLIGHT TO MARS   JUNGLELAND
   SKY DIVE   TUNNEL OF LOVE
         SUBMARINE SANDWICH
            GO-KART RALLY

Geronimo plucked Chris's sleeve.

"On the left, *choonday*. Penny Arcade."

A black-mustached man was coming out. One glimpse of his face told the story. He was pale and sweating—glassy-eyed with fear.

The two TEEN agents dawdled near a cotton-candy machine to watch. The man hurried on with a furtive glance over his shoulder. He kept to the brightly lighted center of the midway, doing his best to lose himself in the throng.

Two men came out of the arcade, heading in the same direction. One, bullnecked with tiny raisin eyes, wore a tight blue-serge suit and wide-brimmed hat. The other, in a trench coat, was bareheaded. They moved with the unhurried air of jungle beasts stalking easy prey. The bull-necked man was chewing on a toothpick.

"*Deeka,*" said Chris. "Let's go."

The boys followed, a dozen paces behind. Presently the two hoods veered off to watch a couple who were popping ducks in a shooting gallery. Their quarry had stopped at a soft-drink stand across from the Fun House.

"Keep going," Chris muttered.

The boys circled to the farther counter of the pop stand, opposite the side on which the man with the black mustache was standing. Chris and Geronimo watched him across the open booth. His hand was shaking and he was having trouble getting his glass of ginger ale up to his mouth without spilling it.

The man's eyes flitted over the passing crowd and the faces around the counter. His gaze met Chris's and suddenly "locked on" as the blond youth rubbed his left eye. Chris yawned. The man's lips trembled in speechless relief.

Chris wiped two fingers across the counter, indicating the two goons. Then he tilted his head toward the Fun House. The man nodded imperceptibly. He eyed Chris's copper-skinned companion and walked off across the midway.

Chris and Geronimo stayed with their Cokes.

In a moment they saw Bullneck and Trench Coat stroll toward the Fun House.

"Which'll it be, Redskin?" Chris murmured.

"The big one with the toothpick."

The Fun House was fronted with grotesque comic faces. In the open mouth of one face was the ticket window. The two hoods paid their admission and disappeared through the bead-curtained entrance. Chris and Geronimo bought tickets and followed them inside to a hall of trick mirrors.

Bullneck and Trench Coat were already out of sight. The TEEN agents hurried after them into a dim passageway. It curved crazily. The floorboards began to sink and hump like ocean waves under their tread. Chris stepped on a whirling disk that almost spun him off his feet.

The passage grew darker. Hanging cobwebs brushed their faces. At times the boys had to stoop or sidle along to avoid obstacles.

"Crazy white men!" Geronimo muttered.

Chris grinned. Suddenly a shriek pierced the air, then a long ghastly wail. Chris felt a pang of alarm. Had they lagged too far behind?

"Snap it up!" he told his partner.

The passageway seemed to widen out. A dangling skeleton and gruesome mummy heads glowed palely in the darkness. Heavy objects like piled sandbags made an obstacle course ahead.

Chris took a pen from his sports coat, plucked off the cap, and held it up to one eye. Through the snooperscope he could make out the reddish ghostly forms of the two hoods, groping their way around opposite walls of the room to the exit.

Chris headed left—his fingers encountering slimy, clammy objects along the wall. Chains clanked and another scream echoed weirdly.

With his scope Chris zeroed in quickly on the man in the trench coat. One last quick glimpse showed the thug whirling around anxiously as he heard a movement behind him. His hand came out of his pocket clutching a weapon.

Chris leaped forward and struck swiftly. His open hand chopped downward in a paralyzing karate blow to the man's forearm. There was a groan of pain, and a metal object clattered to the floor. A savate kick to the jaw finished him off.

Chris beamed a flashlight over the unconscious gunman. He frisked him deftly but found nothing of interest. Through the darkness came faint grunting, scuffling noises, followed by a gasp.

The TEEN agents rejoined each other at the blue-lighted exit. Geronimo was straightening his tie. His teeth gleamed in a wide grin.

"All set?" Chris asked.

"Most delightful fellow," said Geronimo.

At the end of the maze, the boys scrambled out through a huge revolving barrel, then got dumped down a chute to the final exit—a cagelike room barred from floor to ceiling. A few bars were rubber. Chris and Geronimo squirmed outside.

The man with the black mustache was sitting on one of the midway benches.

"Let's play it safe," Chris muttered. "He may have another tail besides those two goons."

The boys walked past him to the shooting gallery. Geronimo bought a round of shots and began knocking down targets with an offhand ease that made the owner's eyes pop worriedly.

Presently their contact got up and strolled off toward the wooded picnic area at one end of the park. Chris scanned the throng keenly.

"All clear," he reported under his breath.

Geronimo laid down his rifle and waved away the cheap souvenir which the owner offered. "Ugh! Injun no like white man's trade junk."

Still wary, the boys approached the picnic area by a roundabout route. Dusk had fallen, but the tables were deserted and they could pick out the man with the mustache clearly enough. He was waiting near a clump of shrubbery.

A stifled cry broke from his lips. The spot was too far from the midway for anyone but the TEEN agents to hear. The man seemed to be writhing and shivering frantically. He started to run—but the impulse carried him only two or three steps before he stumbled and collapsed.

Chris would have darted to assist him. Geronimo grabbed his roommate's arm.

"Iltse, choonday! Watch it, buddy!"

He pulled Chris into the shadows. They peered through the gathering twilight. Was the man ill, or had some unseen assassin struck him down?

A siren wailed in the distance. It drew closer, swelling to a deafening shriek, then stopped as if the police car or ambulance, whatever it was, had turned into the park. The midway throng began surging toward the Fun House.

"Someone must've stumbled on our two playmates," Chris whispered.

They could detect no movement in the picnic area. The hubbub was drawing all attention to the other side of the park. The boys circled among the trees to the figure on the ground.

As they rolled him over, Chris gasped. The man felt freezing cold! In the glow of Geronimo's flashlight they saw why. His clothes, skin, and hair were coated with frost!

"Ai!" Geronimo blurted in a shaken voice. "What has happened to him?"

The face was blue with cold, and his black mustache had come askew. Chris peeled it off.

In the man's pockets were two passports. One bore a photograph that showed him disguised with the fake mustache. It was made out to "John Lee."

The other passport showed him clean-shaven. Chris read the name and gave a low whistle.

"He is Ivor Anson—the missing agent!"

2 · Assignment in Paris

THE BLACK JAGUAR came into Manhattan through
the Lincoln Tunnel and headed uptown through
the Saturday morning traffic.

On Broadway near Fifty-sixth Street stood the
showroom of Luxury Motors, its windows gleaming with expensive foreign sports cars. The Jag
pulled into the service entrance. As Chris and
Geronimo got out, a white-smocked attendant
came bustling up with his clipboard.

"I'd like to speak to the service manager," said
Chris. "Is he in?"

"Right through that door, sir."

The two college students went into an ante-
room where a secretary with honey-colored,
shoulder-length hair was seated at a desk. She

gave them a dazzling smile and pressed a button. The boys went through another door into an elevator.

Chris spoke into an intercom grille: "Kingston One and Two for debriefing."

The cage rose to the top floor. A guard peered at them through a bulletproof-glass port before the elevator door slid open.

The boys went down a carpeted corridor—past the clattering noise of typewriters and teletype machines, past the steel-doored code room and the top-secret Special Projects laboratory—to a flush-paneled door at the end of the hall. An electronic eye sounded a buzzer inside and a green light flashed. The door opened.

"Come in!" Q barked impatiently.

He was sitting hunched at his massive walnut desk with its built-in TV monitor screen. As usual he wore a navy-blue blazer over his open-necked white shirt and a beat-up yachting cap. An unlighted pipe protruded from his thicket of grayish-blond beard, and a half-empty bottle of milk stood close at hand.

Q eyed the boys peevishly. "Rather a nasty little mess you chaps left at the park last night."

"Ulcer bothering you again, sir?" Chris inquired innocently.

Q's face flushed and he started to bellow a reply. But he choked it off and instead poured himself a soothing swig of milk.

The blazer and yachting cap gave him the dashing air of a retired Royal Navy skipper. Chris and Geronimo suspected that he had never commanded anything larger than a canoe in Central Park. For the hundredth time they wondered who Q *really* was. More than once the boys had debated whether even the beard might not be false.

"How's Anson doing, sir?" Chris asked.

"Still in the hospital." Q wiped the milk off his whiskers and sat back. "He's recovered consciousness and the medics say he'll live, but the poor beggar's out of his mind. Can't tell us a thing. . . . His nose and fingers were frostbitten, by the way."

"Any theories on that?"

"None worth wasting my breath on."

Geronimo said, "What about the two gunmen?"

"They won't talk. Cloak and Dagger's still working on them, of course—truth serum, hypnosis, that sort of thing. The general impression is that they've been given mind-blotting treatment—which might point to TOAD."

The boys exchanged startled glances. TOAD was the most feared and fiendish secret organization in the world. As a criminal setup aimed at eventual world domination it outmuscled all known gangs. Its intelligence network at times rivaled the Russian KGB or American CIA.

"Are we allowed to know what sort of job Anson was on, sir?" Chris asked.

"It seems you'll *have* to know." Q got up from his desk to pace the floor. "Anson was sent to France to gather information on a revolutionary new secret weapon. The device is called *Ciel Assassin*—or in English 'Skykill.' "

"Who has it, sir?" put in Geronimo.

"We've no idea. What it does, how it works, who invented it are all unknown. But according to the wild rumors that have filtered through, this thing could change the balance of power in the cold war."

Chris inquired, "Have they backtracked on Anson?"

Q nodded and chewed on his pipe. "He flew in from Paris yesterday morning on that fake passport. Don't ask me why. One guess is that he picked up some information so hot he didn't even dare pass it back through the Paris station of the CIA—another is that something frightened him into a complete panic—maybe both."

"And where do we fit in, sir?"

"Cloak and Dagger wants one of our teams sent over to sniff out the situation. Since you two contacted Anson, you seem to be the natural choice."

Spring vacation in Paris! Chris managed to suppress a grin of delight. "How much do we have to go on, sir?"

"Little enough. Anson was a lone wolf—had his own way of operating. It seems he had wide contacts in the French underworld and used the code name 'Omega' when buying information from tipsters and stool pigeons. Apparently that was how he first picked up a lead on Skykill."

"Does the CIA have any idea what sort of a lead it was?"

Q shook his head. "None. However, there is one other clue."

He opened a drawer, took out a roll of canvas, and spread it on the desk. The canvas bore an oil painting—the portrait of a dark-haired girl.

"This was sewn into Anson's coat lining."

Chris made out the artist's signature. "Triquet. Has the CIA checked on that name?"

"They've tried, but none of the art collectors here in New York has ever heard of him. Didn't recognize the style, either."

"May we have a copy of this?"

"Photographic prints have already been made. Pomeroy will give each of you one. You're to see him before you leave here, of course."

Pomeroy was the chief of TEEN's technical staff—sometimes referred to as "The Department of Dirty Tricks." He was a fussy, baldheaded little genius who outfitted all TEEN agents with their electronic gadgetry and other special equipment.

"How soon do we leave, sir?" Geronimo asked.

"Tomorrow night. Two seats have been booked on an Air France flight to Paris."

On Sunday evening the helicopter bus deposited the boys at Kennedy International Airport. They checked in at the Air France ticket counter, picked two seats off the chart, and went upstairs to the lounge.

At last the loudspeaker announced their flight. The boys filed aboard the huge transatlantic jet with the other passengers. A stewardess hung their raincoats on the wardrobe rack and showed them to their seats. Geronimo took the window and Chris slid in beside him.

The seats were three abreast. Presently a girl was ushered to the aisle seat next to Chris. Geronimo murmured the Apache equivalent of "quite a dish."

"You're not being sent on this war party to admire squaws," Chris replied in the same language. "I'll handle all that."

The girl's pale-blond hair was cut in a short, boyish style. Her face looked tense and unhappy.

"Care to sit by the window?"

The girl seemed startled by Chris's question. Her slightly slanted violet eyes flashed over him. Chris had a sudden disturbing hunch that he had seen her somewhere before. "*Non*—thank you, monsieur—I am quite comfortable," she said in a thick French accent and turned away.

Chris racked his brain, trying to place her. It was a minute or so before he clued in. Her hair had been dyed and cut shorter than in the oil painting found on Anson!

He took out the print, studied it furtively, and held it toward Geronimo. "She's sitting next to me," he said in Apache.

Geronimo looked her over impassively. "I don't like this, *choonday*. How come she flies on the same plane and camps right next to us, eh?"

"Just a lucky chance maybe."

The girl showed no desire to become friendly. Even after take-off, when dinner was being served, she evaded all of Chris's conversational ploys.

At last the lights were dimmed and the passengers settled back as the jet streaked high over the Atlantic.

The girl seemed restless and nervous. She leafed through a number of magazines the stewardess brought and finally went forward to choose another from the magazine rack.

Chris watched her through narrowed eyes. As she was coming back, a man's hand suddenly reached out from an aisle seat and grabbed her arm! Chris saw her eyes widen in terror. She jerked free and hurried on to her seat.

"Was he annoying you?" Chris asked.

"*Non!* N-not at all, monsieur! It was nothing. I think he mistook me for someone else."

Chris waited a while. Then he excused himself and went forward to get a magazine. On the way back, he studied the man in the aisle seat. He was a squat, blubber-lipped type and his head seemed to grow directly out of his shoulders. Chris remembered seeing this man at the boarding gate. His bulging, heavy-lidded eyes stared back at the TEEN agent, then closed slowly.

The boys snatched a brief sleep. It was scarcely midnight, New York time, when the lights were turned up again and the stewards and stewardesses began to serve breakfast.

Presently the captain's voice announced, "Good morning, *mesdames et messieurs!* We shall land at Orly Airport in half an hour. The weather is warm and sunny—a perfect day for your arrival in Paris!"

There was steady traffic to the rest room as the passengers freshened up. Finally the jet landed. Everyone stood up and began filing slowly aft to disembark. Chris and Geronimo retrieved their raincoats from the rack.

Chris shrugged on his coat, slid his hands into the pockets, and experienced a shock of surprise. There was something odd in the right-hand pocket. Something moist, slimy—and *alive.*

He pulled it out slowly and saw the sentence of doom in his hand. It was a wriggling, blinking toad—the repulsive and sinister warning sent to all of TOAD's intended victims!

3 · Café Stakeout

CHRIS SHUDDERED AS the toad squirmed in his hand. Who had slipped it into his coat pocket? The girl? The squat, heavy-lidded man? Either might have done it on a trip to the rest room.

Or was there some unknown enemy aboard—someone who had spotted him as a TEEN agent?

Chris grinned coldly as his eye fell on a black-and-white-checked topcoat. He had seen the heavy-lidded man wearing it back at Kennedy. Chris's hand moved casually and deposited the toad in the closest pocket of the topcoat. Behind him, Geronimo began humming an Apache war chant.

"You saw?" Chris asked over his shoulder.

"I saw."

The boys followed the stream of passengers into the huge terminal and through passport control. As they went to claim their luggage, Chris's eyes roved around, keeping the blond girl and the heavy-lidded man in view.

"We'll each follow one of them," he told his partner. Chris flipped a coin. "Heads for the blond, tails for Frogface."

"Okay, I'll take the toss," said Geronimo.

Chris uncovered the coin—tails up. "We'll meet at the hotel later," he said.

The boys got their suitcases and hurried on to the customs counters. Several lines were forming. Chris managed to slip in behind the girl.

Presently he saw the squat, heavy-lidded man enter an adjoining line. The bulging eyes shot a venomous glance at Chris, who smiled back pleasantly.

"Anything to declare, monsieur?" the customs man asked.

"Nothing," Chris replied, and was waved on. He grabbed the bag and strode out of the terminal. The blond was climbing into a Peugeot 404 taxicab. As it pulled away from the curb, her gaze swept over the TEEN agent.

Chris hailed the next cab in line and told the driver to follow the Peugeot. They swung out into the fast flow of traffic roaring northward into Paris. Chris kept watch out the back window but could see no sign he was being tailed.

The driver eyed him in the rear-view window. "*Êtes-vous Français*, monsieur?"

"No. American."

"Ah! Yet you speak the language very well."

"Thanks."

"This blond morsel in the Peugeot—she is your sweetheart? You have had the disagreement?"

"No chance—yet." Chris grinned. "Let's just say I'd like to get better acquainted."

"*Mais certainement!* It is springtime in Paris, eh?" The driver blew a kiss from his fingertips. "I promise you, she shall not escape us!"

The traffic raced into the city up the Avenue d'Italie. Chris's pulse beat faster as he savored the sights and sounds and scents of Paris—the wide, leafy boulevards with chestnut trees in full bloom, the colorful news kiosks, policemen in capes directing traffic or pedaling along on bicycles. Store shutters were being rolled up for the day's business.

The Peugeot turned left on the Boulevard de Port-Royal and sped into Montparnasse, the famed artists' quarter. It stopped before an ancient-looking stone apartment building and Chris saw the blond girl get out.

His own taxi pulled over to the curb farther down the block. Chris slipped the driver a generous tip. "Take my things to the Hotel l'Empereur, will you, please? My name's on the tag—Christopher Cool."

He crossed the street and walked back to a café on the corner, pausing to buy a morning paper at the newsstand. Inside the café, people on their way to work were snatching hasty breakfasts of coffee and croissants. Chris took a table by the window, ordered *café au lait,* and kept one eye on the apartment house across the street.

By the time he had browsed through the paper twice, the waiter had begun setting up tables and chairs on the sidewalk outside. Chris moved out into the sunshine. Over his third glass of *café au lait* he continued to keep a watchful eye on the apartment. Still no sign of the girl.

Gradually the tables began to fill up. Some of the customers were ordinary Parisian workaday types. Others looked like artists or students.

A burly, muscular young man in a turtle-neck jersey took a table next to Chris's. He had a bristling beard, shaggy dark mane, and piercing eyes, which fixed Chris in a steady gaze. Chris remained unconcerned.

"You are waiting for someone?" the man finally asked in a needling voice.

"Perhaps."

"Maybe you would like my company better, eh?"

Chris shrugged.

The fellow grinned insultingly. "You smell like an American to me—*cochon.*"

Chris grinned.

"I just called you a pig."

"I'm afraid I don't hear very well."

"Then I will say it again, louder—*cochon!*"

The waiter hovered closer, flicking his towel nervously. Chris smiled and went on sipping.

The man's face darkened. Suddenly his huge hand lashed out to knock the glass from Chris's lips. Instead, it met empty air as Chris flung the coffee in his face. At the same time, Chris's foot extended to jerk the rung of his opponent's chair. The man landed with a hard thump on the sidewalk.

He picked himself up, livid with rage and dripping coffee. A knife flashed from under his pant leg as he lunged at Chris. What followed was like a fast, graceful ballet.

Chris swept up the metal-legged table and caught the knife in the wooden top. Before his assailant could let go the hilt, Chris yanked the table aside, pulling him off-balance. Suddenly Chris assumed the *kiba-dachi* stance. Pivoting on his left foot, he drove his right elbow hard into the pit of his foe's stomach.

The man gasped and crumpled as the café customers watched in silent fascination. The waiter bustled up and the proprietor came hurrying out of the café in shirt sleeves and apron.

"I saw it all. This one was asking for it," the waiter assured his boss, nudging the fallen man with his foot.

"Shall I call *les flics,* monsieur?" the proprietor asked Chris.

"I am sure we both prefer not to be bothered by the police," Chris said.

The café owner splashed water in the fellow's face and they helped him to his feet. He gave Chris a stunned look and staggered off. In a few moments Chris was seated at his table again, peacefully sipping a fresh *café au lait.*

"I applaud your most skillful handling of an unpleasant situation, monsieur," said a voice.

Chris looked around. One of the customers had come over—a tall, skinny, mummified-looking man with wavy gray hair. He was elegantly dressed in a pin-striped suit with long pointed lapels and a pearl stickpin. On one arm hung a cane, and he was carrying a Homburg hat and gloves.

Chris smiled and offered him a chair.

"Merci, monsieur." The dummy sat down, plucked a calling card from his wallet, and handed it to Chris.

The card read *Alexandre Valaud, Dealer in Objets d'Art,* and gave a phone number and address on the Boul Mich.

"I'm afraid I haven't a card of my own. My name is Chris Cool."

Valaud smiled, showing long yellow teeth, and gave Chris a quick, cold-fish handshake.

"I am an art dealer, as you see, and quite

wealthy. Unfortunately I have made a number of enemies—business enemies, you comprehend? Tiresome fools who accuse me of cheating them simply because my wits and artistic judgment are sharper than their own. From time to time, several have attacked me or tried to kill me."

Chris made sympathetic noises.

Valaud went on, "I need a bodyguard. The pay would be excellent—two thousand francs a week and all expenses. Would you be interested, Monsieur Cool?"

Chris shook his head regretfully. "Thanks, but no. I'm an American, over here on vacation."

Valaud's murky green eyes studied the slender college boy. Then he arose and bowed. "If you should change your mind, monsieur, the offer will still be open." Again they shook hands.

Valaud donned his hat and strolled off stiffly but jauntily with his cane.

Chris settled back and returned his gaze to the apartment building. More than likely it had a rear entrance. Was there still any hope of the girl showing herself, especially if it was she who had sent the bearded man as Chris suspected?

He decided to hang on until lunchtime. By then if there was still no sign of the blond, he would go over and have a short chat with the *concierge* of her apartment house.

Twenty minutes later his pulse quickened as the girl came out the front door. Chris made his way across the street through the darting traffic.

The blond was heading north toward the Boulevard du Montparnasse. Chris followed. Her steps grew slower. After a block or so, she stopped in front of the window of a *boulangerie* filled with freshly baked bread and pastries, and suddenly whirled around. Chris walked toward her.

"Why are you following me?" Her pretty face contorted in a mixture of anger and fear. "What is it you want?"

"For one thing, I'd like to know why you sicced your bearded friend on me at the café."

The blond seemed flustered by the unexpected accusation. "I—I only did it because you trailed me from the airport, monsieur, and then planted yourself across the street from my apartment. It is not pleasant to be hounded!"

Chris shifted to the Sir Galahad approach. "I'm sorry, mademoiselle. On the plane I sensed that you were in trouble—afraid of something. I only wanted to help."

The girl stared at Chris as if she wanted to believe him but did not dare. Suddenly her violet eyes brimmed with tears. "Oh, monsieur," she sobbed, "if only you knew! I have been living in absolute terror these past few days!"

Her voice had the ring of truth. "Is there anything I can do?" Chris asked gently.

The girl dabbed her eyes and nose. *"Eh bien!* If you really wish to help, you can do so."

She hesitated a moment. "You see, before I went to America, someone turned over to me a priceless painting to—to keep safe. That is how the trouble began."

"What sort of painting?" Chris asked.

"I have it hidden, but if you come with me, I will show it to you."

She hailed a taxi and gave the driver directions. After a crawling ride eastward through the noon-day traffic, he deposited them on the Quai St. Bernard, overlooking the River Seine by the Botanical Gardens.

The girl led Chris down a flight of stone steps to a houseboat barge moored near the Austerlitz Bridge. "The painting is hidden aboard."

"Perhaps you'd better go first and show me."

She gave him a reproachful look but did not argue. Clambering onto the barge, she led the way past tarry coils of rope into the deckhouse.

Chris followed, ducking his head as he passed through the low doorway. This proved to be a serious mistake. Something struck him hard on the back of the skull. Dazzling fireworks exploded in his brain, then faded out slowly into ringing darkness as he collapsed.

4 · A Cold Calling Card

CHRIS STRUGGLED FOR breath. He was floating, squirming, kicking in some liquid green nightmare. His lungs felt ready to burst, but when he opened his mouth or tried to inhale, what came in was water—not air.

Somehow the will to live drove him upward. He broke surface, gulping frantically. Where was he? In the Seine, of course.

He trod water, fighting down waves of sickness that threatened to turn his stomach inside out. The current was carrying him downstream toward the Pont Sully and the southern tip of the Ile St. Louis. On the quay to his left lay the great wine warehouse of the Halle Aux Vins.

One of the glassed-in excursion boats that ply

the Seine had just glided past, loaded with passengers. A tug was towing a string of barges downriver. Near the Sully Bridge he could see a pair of fishermen.

The idiots! he groaned. Couldn't anyone spot a drowning man?

Rather than waste energy shouting, Chris struck out for shore. He made it finally with his last ounce of strength. Dragging himself out of the water, he flopped onto the stone quay.

For a while his whole frame was shaken by spasms of retching. The fit left him weak, but got most of the water out.

After a time Chris sat up and allowed the sun to warm and dry him a bit. The houseboat was still lying moored upstream near the Pont d'Austerlitz—not that there was much chance the blond and her boy friend would still be hanging around.

He walked back along the quay. As expected, the houseboat was empty. On closer inspection, it looked as if it had not been used in some time. Painted in fading letters at the stern was the name *Liliane, Ostende*.

No doubt whoever slugged Chris had simply picked the empty boat as a convenient trap. If the bearded man were the assailant he could have got to the river fast via the Métro, the Paris subway, then phoned the girl and baited the trap. Or was TOAD behind the attack?

"Well, no use standing around with tadpoles coming out of my ears," Chris said to himself. "Better get out of these wet clothes first, and see if Redskin Buddy has anything to report."

He took a taxi to the Hotel l'Empereur on the Rue St. Jacques in the Latin Quarter. TEEN had picked it as a likely student spot, since it was near the Sorbonne, heart of the University of Paris.

As he registered at the hotel desk, Chris asked if his friend Geronimo had arrived yet and was told that he had not. The concierge gave a slight cough.

"You look a bit damp, monsieur."

Chris grinned. "Yes, I fell in the Seine."

The man raised his eyebrows and shrugged as if to say, "These crazy Americans!"

Chris showered and changed into his crisp poplin suit, then cashed a traveler's check and took a taxi to the blond's apartment house.

The concierge who answered the door buzzer was a gaunt, horse-faced woman with dangling earrings and a brassy yellow fright wig. Chris described the blond girl to her.

"There are many blond people who live here, monsieur," she said coldly. "I myself am a blond."

Chris tried some flattery. "The one I am looking for, madame, was not so stately and handsome as yourself, but perhaps three or four years younger—say twenty-two at the most. She sat next to me on a plane from America this morning."

"Ah, *mais oui!* You mean Mademoiselle Dubois—Brigitte Dubois. But, alas, she moved out just an hour ago."

Chris mentally chewed himself out for not having gone straight back to the apartment from the quay. "Mademoiselle Dubois left some forwarding address, perhaps?"

The woman shook her dangling earrings. "I am sorry, monsieur. She told me nothing."

Chris ate a late lunch at a nearby restaurant and pondered his next move. At least he was in the right part of Paris for finding out something about Triquet.

He began in an art-supply shop in the Rue Delambre. The dealer could tell him nothing. On other streets Chris had no better luck. He began working his way north into the St. Germain des Prés neighborhood, which he knew was full of art galleries. The proprietors were eager to interest him in promising young painters, but none knew Triquet.

Chris was beginning to get tired of the name. He stopped at a café for a cool drink. As he took out his wallet to pay, his eye fell on Alexandre Valaud's card, still slightly sodden from its dip in the Seine.

On a sudden impulse Chris purchased some telephone tokens from the cashier and inquired for a phone booth.

"Downstairs, monsieur, next to the rest room."

A secretary answered the call. Chris gave his name and a moment later Valaud came on the line. "Ah! You have changed your mind?"

"I'm afraid not, sir. Just wanted to ask if you'd ever heard of a painter named Triquet."

"Triquet? Let me see. The name is familiar, *certainement*. . . . Yes, of course—Triquet! Not too promising an artist, I fear. You are interested in seeing his work?"

"No, sir, but I'd like to get in touch with him. Can you tell me where he lives?"

"I have never met this Triquet, but the information you need should be in my files. A moment, please."

Presently Valaud returned with the address. Chris thanked him and caught a taxi outside.

The place proved to be a narrow stone tenement building on a dingy street near the Quai St. Michel. The front door stood ajar. Chris's nostrils were assailed by stale cooking odors of boiled cabbage and garlic. There was no sign of a concierge, but he glimpsed an elderly man in an undershirt down the hall.

"Triquet?"

"Top floor, monsieur. Last door on the right."

Chris climbed the rickety stairs to the garret. Outside Triquet's door lay a small block of ice. Chris knocked.

"Who is it?" a voice called.

"Un ami," he whispered hoarsely.

The bearded fellow who had been at the café that morning peered out. He gaped in dismay and tried to slam the door, but Chris's foot had already been jammed in the opening. His hand snaked through and grabbed the beard.

"Open up—*cochon!*" To emphasize his order, Chris gave the beard a sharp yank, and the door opened smartly. Chris stepped inside.

It was a typical artist's studio, littered with canvases and pots of paint. A skylight sloped almost to the floor. Brigitte Dubois was standing near a curtain at one side of the room, evidently used to partition off the living quarters from the artist's work space. She stared at Chris with wide, fearful eyes.

Triquet growled, "It is against the law to break in."

"It's also against the law to slug people and dump them in the Seine. However, if you like, I can call the police and have you both arrested."

Triquet and Brigitte exchanged worried glances.

"Who are you?" the blond asked Chris. "Can't you get it through your head that I do not wish your help! What is it you want?"

"I'll ask the questions, please. Suppose we start by finding out who *you* are. The name is Brigitte Dubois—right?"

The blond gave a sulky nod. "I am a model—an artist's model."

Chris turned to her black-bearded companion. "And you?"

"Paul Triquet. You have eyes. I am a painter, as you see. Brigitte is my cousin. You were pestering her and she needed help to get rid of you, so I did what I could."

"What were you doing in America?" Chris asked Brigitte.

"I went there to . . . to see a friend."

"Who?"

"I—I will not tell you, monsieur." Her violet eyes wavered under Chris's cold stare and she bit her lower lip nervously. "Anyhow, his name can be of no importance to you. I was there only one day and then came back because he—my friend— was taken ill."

"Interesting coincidence. I have a friend who was recently taken ill, too—and he happened to be carrying a painting of you, Mademoiselle Dubois."

Brigitte's eyes widened again. "Ivor Anson?"

Chris nodded.

"Are you a . . . a secret agent, monsieur?"

"Sure, 007 himself." Chris grinned sarcastically. "It happens I'm a college student on vacation, but I intend to find out why Anson was—taken ill, as you put it. So let's cut out the sparring. Who was that creep on the plane last night who grabbed your arm?"

"I do not know—believe me, monsieur! But it is true I had seen him before."

"Where?"

"Here. In Paris. He had been spying on Ivor—I mean, Monsieur Anson—for several days before Anson flew home to the United States."

"Anson was frightened about something?"

"*Oui,* monsieur. Very frightened. With good reason as it turned out."

"Of what?"

"Of the same thing—the same person that has me terrified, too." Brigitte's voice had sunk to a husky whisper. "A person whom Ivor knew only as *Le Glacier*—The Iceman. Or sometimes he spoke of him as The Chiller."

A picture rose in Chris's memory of Anson lying on the picnic ground blue with cold, his skin frosted with tiny scales of—

Suddenly Chris remembered something else. "Have you seen what's lying outside your door?" he said, glancing from Brigitte to Triquet.

"What do you mean, monsieur?" the artist asked.

They followed as Chris strode back to the door and opened it. The ice was still there, but it had melted to little more than a cube.

Brigitte's face went ashen when she saw it. She swayed weakly and would have collapsed if Triquet had not caught her. His own face looked sick.

Chris himself felt oddly woozy. It was a moment before the answer hit him—vapor, deadly vapor from the melting ice!

He snatched it up and raced to the skylight. Flinging a pane wide open, he hurled the ice cube outside.

Chris was just turning back to Brigitte and Triquet when a deafening blast shook the studio!

5 · The Chiller

THE EXPLOSION SHATTERED the skylight and sent
a shower of broken glass to the floor. Brigitte
and Triquet were at a safe distance near the door,
but all three were knocked off their feet.

They lay stunned but uninjured.

"*Nom de bleu!*" gasped Triquet in a shaky
voice. "What happened?"

They picked themselves up, surprised to be
alive.

"Evidently the ice was more lethal than I
thought," said Chris.

"Then you did not know it would explode?"

Chris shook his head. "It contained a layer of
frozen poison gas—cyanogen or hydrogen cyanide
probably. The stuff vaporized as the ice melted.

That's what was making us ill. In time it would have seeped in under the door. But the center of the ice cube must have contained some nitroglycerin, too."

"Nitro!" Triquet's face again turned sickly pale. "You mean—the stuff for blowing safes?"

"I'm afraid so. Doesn't take much to set it off. Just the shaking-up from being thrown out the window was enough."

"And if you hadn't thrown it out—?"

Chris shrugged. "When the ice melted, the nitro would have dribbled along the floor, I suppose. And you would have stepped on it, coming out of your apartment."

Triquet's hand was trembling as he wiped the beads of perspiration from his forehead. Brigitte sank down on a chair.

"Le Glacier!" she quavered fearfully. "He is out to get me, too—just as he got Ivor!"

The panic in her eyes gave Chris the feeling that she was ready to reveal everything. He peered out the broken skylight for a moment at the street below. Knots of people had gathered and heads were sticking out of windows, but apparently no one had been hurt by the blast.

"How well did you know Anson?" Chris asked.

"We were engaged to be married, as soon as he finished his . . . his mission here in France." Seeing Chris's narrowed glance, she added hastily, "He was a secret agent, of course. Oh yes, I know that very well, monsieur—and I think you know it, too."

"What happened? I mean, why did Anson go back to the United States?"

"To save his life!" Brigitte blurted impatiently. "As I told you, he was in deadly fear. He knew that the Chiller was hunting him. Three times he had the most narrow escape—and there was no place left to hide. He knew that next time would mean the finish."

"You went back to America with him?"

"*Non.* He flew back by himself—in disguise. I was to follow on a different flight and join him in New York. But I arrived too late."

Brigitte's voice choked. "On Saturday when I landed, there was a newspaper story telling that a man named John Lee had been found in a park . . . his mind blank, unable to talk. What was the use of seeing him? I knew if I tried, I might be the Chiller's next victim. So I flew home again to Paris."

"Who is the Chiller?" Chris asked. "Don't you know anything about him?"

"Nothing—except that he is deadly and has eyes everywhere. When you trailed me from the airport, monsieur, I feared that you might be one of his agents. That is why I phoned my cousin to help get rid of you. But at the café you proved not so easy to deal with—so we faked up that story of the valuable painting."

"What about the man on the plane—that frog-faced character? Could he be the Chiller?"

"*Non.*" Brigitte shook her head. "I am sure he is not *Le Glacier*, or Ivor would have known. But Ivor feared he might be working for *Le Glacier* —and I, too, fear him for the same reason."

Chris went back to the broken skylight. "There's a way we might find out what's behind all this," he said after a moment.

"What do you mean, monsieur?"

"Whoever planted that ice outside the door may still be watching the building."

"You see someone down there?" Brigitte's face paled.

"Hard to tell from here," Chris said. "But if you and I left together, we might get him to show himself—assuming anyone *is* watching."

"*Non!* I will not do it!" Brigitte's voice throbbed with fear. "It is too dangerous—to turn our backs and let him follow us. He might strike us down from behind!"

"Don't worry. He won't take us unaware. I promise you that." Seeing her stubborn expression, Chris added, "Look! Do you want to go on living like this, in fear of your life? You've both just had one narrow escape. Next time you may not be so lucky. This is a chance to get him off your back, once and for all."

Brigitte looked uncertainly at Triquet.

The painter gave a worried shrug. "I do not

know, *ma chère*. Maybe he is right. Somehow I think this fellow knows what he is talking about."

Brigitte took a deep breath. "*Eh bien,*" she said to Chris. "I will do what you say."

"Good."

They watched as Chris took out a pair of dark sunglasses with large, square eyeframes.

"You think the *lunettes de soleil* make a clever disguise?" she asked with biting scorn.

"No, but they give me two-way vision—forward and also in back, if I turn my head slightly. Half of each lens is a rear-view mirror. They pick up an image from a prism at each hinge."

"Ah-h-h, *je comprends!*"

Moments later Chris and the blond emerged from the tenement house. A knot of people was jabbering at two policemen. The couple walked down the block and turned left at the corner. Across the street was an open-air café.

Through his rear-view glasses, Chris saw a man leave one of the tables and start in pursuit.

Chris and Brigitte continued without speeding their pace. The shadower was following, half a block behind. He wore a beret, and a dark open-necked sport shirt under his tweed jacket.

"Left again at the next corner," Chris murmured.

As soon as they had turned out of sight of their shadow, Chris broke step abruptly and pushed Brigitte against the shopwindow. It was a little *tabac,* surmounted by the red lantern-like emblem of all Paris tobacco stores.

Brigitte was trembling. "What are you going to do?" she whispered.

"Sh-h-h!" Chris took off his sunglasses.

Presently their shadow came around the corner. He had the dark-skinned, Arab look of an Algerian. His jaw dropped in dismay as Chris suddenly stepped in front of him.

"May we help you, *mon ami?*" Chris smiled.

The Algerian snarled and backed off, his hand snatching at his coat pocket. A knife had barely flashed into view when Chris leaped up and kicked it from his hand. Catlike, Chris pivoted and met the Algerian head-on, with a hand-sword karate jab to the chest.

The stunning force sent the man reeling. In blind panic, he turned and fled.

"*Allons-y!*" Chris shouted and darted after him, Brigitte following as fast as she could.

Startled pedestrians impeded the chase. Chris dodged them quarterback-style, trying not to lose sight of his quarry.

A blue Citroen DS was parked near the café. The Algerian dived into it and clawed at the ignition. Chris reached the car just as its engine came to life. He grabbed wildly at the door handle, but the Citroen roared off.

A taxicab was coming from the opposite direction. Chris hailed it with a yell. Brigitte was just catching up as the taxi U-turned. He pushed her into it ahead of him and shouted orders to the driver.

"A hundred francs if you can catch that Citroen!"

It was heading for the Boulevard St. Michel, but the late-afternoon heavy traffic blocked its getaway. Turning north, the Citroen bored its way across the Ile de la Cité to the Right Bank. Chris hunched grimly behind the driver, watching.

The Citroen traced a zigzag course, turning into side streets, then doubling back in a vain attempt to shake them. Chris's taxi hung on like a bulldog to a burglar's pant leg.

The rush-hour snarl was growing worse—a typical Paris traffic jam—as people headed home to dinner. Lively French insults were traded out the car windows. The Citroen was soon wedged in too tightly to escape—but its pursuer, by the same token, was unable to overhaul it and force it to the curb.

As they crawled up the Champs Élysées, the western sky was reddening behind the Arc de Triomphe. The Citroen circled and headed east again. Later they crossed back to the Left Bank.

"*Zut alors!*" Brigitte fumed nervously. "We are on a sightseeing tour of Paris!"

"He could have been on the open highway by now," Chris agreed. An uneasy suspicion was

growing in his mind. Perhaps the Algerian was
killing time on purpose—leading them on an in-
tentional wild-goose chase.

At last the Citroen swung left off the Avenue de
la Bourdonnais. It was halting near the base of
the Eiffel Tower! The Algerian jumped out and
ran toward the ticket booth.

Chris's taxi was held up at the turn. By the time
it reached the tower, the Algerian was entering
one of the Eiffel elevators. Chris shoved money
into the taximan's hand and ran to intercept the
fugitive. Too late! The cage was starting upward.

"Rats!"

Grabbing Brigitte's arm Chris turned back to
the ticket booth. It was minutes before the next
elevator ascended.

Chris was sweating with frustration and im-
patience as the cage rose through the iron grill-
work of the tower leg. He would have to search
all three platforms. Meanwhile, the Algerian
might be on his way down again.

The man was nowhere on the first sightseeing
level, either inside the glass-enclosed restaurant
or on the open platform. At the second level Chris
also drew a blank.

He entered the elevator cage again with Brigitte for the long ride up to the top level at the
tower peak. The view was breathtaking. The
whole panorama of Paris lay spread out below—
even the white dome of the Sacré-Coeur could be

glimpsed on the heights of Montmartre far to the north.

The elevator cage stopped. Chris hurried out, scanning the people scattered around the platform. His quarry stood at the rail. Chris gave a grin of triumph as he recognized the beret and rumpled tweed jacket. He strode toward the man and tapped his shoulder.

"Great view, isn't it?"

The man turned, showing a scar on his right cheek. But he was not the Algerian!

Then Brigitte screamed.

Chris whirled, but not fast enough. The Algerian, in shirt sleeves, grabbed Chris by the coat as the scar-faced man seized the youth's arm.

Together they flung Chris far out over the rail into empty space!

6 · A Fast Getaway

CHRIS'S STOMACH CHURNED as he gazed at the ground and the antlike people almost a thousand feet below. With a sky diver's roll he flipped head-up, then spread his arms and kicked his heels together sharply.

The kick triggered rocket-hoppers in his shoes. With a *whoosh*, compressed CO_2 jetted from his hollow titanium-steel soles and heels, billowing into a cloud of white exhaust.

As the rockets braked Chris's fall, he hovered motionless for a moment, then slowly began to descend.

Suddenly a white line snaked from the tower platform. Geronimo! The Apache must be up there somewhere and had fired the life-line shell carried by all TEEN agents!

The aim was good. Chris grasped the line and swarmed up the slender nylon rope to the tower platform. In moments he was climbing back over the rail, to which the free end of the line was hooked.

The platform was a scene of wild confusion as a guard tried to calm the milling sightseers. "Monsieur! Are you all right?" he cried frantically.

Chris nodded and shouldered his way through the cluster of people. They had gathered around two men who lay sprawled unconscious. One was the Algerian—the other his scar-faced pal!

Chris grinned. Geronimo was on deck, all right!

"*Koya, choonday!* This way!" The Apache was near the elevator, beckoning. He had one arm around Brigitte, who looked ready to faint.

Chris darted to join them. Suddenly from the corner of his eye he saw another figure burst into view. The squat, frog-faced man! His hand went inside his jacket.

Chris's reaction was faster. He snatched out a pen, aimed it, and pressed the clip. Frogface's bulging eyes seemed to go glassy with amazement, then he crumpled in a heap! The "sleepy sliver" of anesthetic would put him out for at least an hour.

The elevator cage rose into view and clanked to a halt. Two guards came rushing out.

"Over there!" Chris said, directing them toward the crowd of people at the rail.

"*Merci,* monsieur!" They dashed past.

The TEEN agents immediately stepped aboard with Brigitte.

"Down, please!" Chris said urgently to the startled operator. "This lady's about to be ill—all the excitement, you understand."

"*Oui,* monsieur!"

At ground level they emerged from the elevator into another excited knot of spectators.

Chris smiled, and hurried off with Brigitte and Geronimo. The important thing now was to clear out before the police arrived. The TEEN agents had no desire to discuss their adventures.

"Come on! We'll use the Algerian's car!" Chris led the way toward the spot where the blue Citroen had been parked, but his eyes suddenly widened.

"It is gone!" Brigitte gasped.

Who had taken it? Chris shot a startled glance at Geronimo, who responded blankly, "Don't look at me, *choonday!*"

A taxi came cruising past. Chris hailed it and the trio got in. Brigitte gave the driver Triquet's address.

On the way, Chris told Geronimo all that had happened. In Apache he explained that Brigitte was Anson's fiancée and that he felt she could be trusted.

Geronimo, in turn, told how he had trailed the frog-faced man.

"He made a quick phone call from the airport," the Indian youth related. "Then he took a taxi to an apartment across the river, up near Clichy. No place for a stakeout, so I had to rent a room across the street. About one o'clock this Algerian character with the beret pulled up in a blue Citroen and went inside."

"What happened?"

"Nothing much. He came out with Frogface and a man with a scar. They ate lunch at a restaurant down the block and then went back to the apartment. Pretty soon the Algerian shoved off, carrying what looked like a hatbox."

"It probably held the explosive hunk of ice, packed in a cushioning arrangement," Chris said.

Geronimo nodded. "That figures. Everything stayed quiet after that till about five-thirty. Then Frogface and the man with the scar came out and hailed a taxi."

"They went straight to the Eiffel Tower?"

"Right. Eventually the Algerian joined them, up on the top platform. I was keeping out of sight on the other side, but I saw him give Scarface his coat and beret. Then you two showed up."

Brigitte shuddered. "It was terrible! Never again do I want to see such a thing, monsieur, as when you were thrown off the tower!"

Geronimo chuckled. "Needless to add, I had to kayo the Algerian and Scarface with a couple of sleepy slivers before I could fire the rescue line."

"What about Frogpuss?" Chris asked.

"He ducked out of sight while I was hooking the line to the railing. I was still trying to spot him when you climbed back aboard."

Chris frowned thoughtfully. "Let's see if we can't put the whole jigsaw together. . . . That phone call from the airport may have alerted the Algerian to be on the lookout for Brigitte. He could even have been watching her place while I was staked out at the café. Then after I got dumped in the Seine, he went back to report to Frogface that Brigitte had moved in with her cousin—which gave them a chance to set up the ice caper."

"What about afterward?" said Brigitte. "How could they foresee that you would chase the Algerian and be led to the Eiffel Tower?"

Chris shook his head. "They couldn't. The Citroen must have had a two-way radio, and he used it to tell Frogface we were tailing him. Then he led us a merry chase around Paris while the other two were getting to the tower."

Chris chewed his lower lip for a moment before going on. "There's another possibility—about the ice, I mean."

"Such as?" Geronimo queried.

"Well, there's no telling how big the piece was to start with, or how fast it would melt. The container was probably insulated, of course, but I've a hunch the ice wasn't placed outside the door till shortly before I arrived."

"Maybe the Algerian had no chance to sneak in and plant it until then."

"Could be," Chris agreed. "Or maybe it was meant for me, rather than Brigitte and Triquet—or maybe for all three of us."

Geronimo looked doubtful. "Doesn't add up. How could they guess you were coming to Triquet's place?"

"Well, it's a long shot, I admit—but if the Algerian saw me get dumped off the houseboat, they may have figured I was bound to come after Triquet, sooner or later."

"Sounds pretty iffy," said Geronimo.

Suddenly Chris snapped his fingers. "Valaud!"

"Who's he?" Geronimo asked.

Chris explained rapidly, adding, "Maybe Valaud is part of Frogface's outfit too. He could have tipped them off after I called to get Triquet's address!"

Chris told their driver to pull over near a sidewalk telephone booth. In Apache he added, "Think I'd better call Uncle Phil and report."

Uncle Phil was the code name for the Paris station of the CIA. Chris dialed the unlisted number and counted five rings—then hung up and dialed again—the signal for an agent's call.

A rather high-pitched man's voice answered. *"Allô?"*

"Uncle Phil?"

"Yes."

"This is Wunny Kingston. Just got into Paris this morning."

"Splendid! Is Tooey with you?"

"Yes, indeed."

"You're coming to visit Aunt Maud and me, aren't you?"

"Not just yet, but I thought I should call you at least. We went sightseeing around town and had quite a thrilling experience up on the Eiffel Tower. Somebody almost fell off and three men fainted. I certainly hope they get looked after promptly, because you never know in cases like that."

"That's very true, my boy. Were they taken to a hospital?"

"Probably—but the police were called, too, I imagine. Another funny thing, one of the men's cars disappeared. I happen to know because he arrived at the tower just ahead of our taxi. It was a blue Citroen DS"—Chris reeled off the license number—"and it was gone when we came down."

"Well, well, that does sound exciting! Have you had any other adventures?"

"Oh, one or two little things. We'll tell you about them when we see you. Meantime, we're thinking about buying some paintings. I wonder if you could tell us whether a man on the Boul

Mich named Alexandre Valaud is a reliable person to deal with."

"Alexandre Valaud?" Uncle Phil said sharply. "Good heavens, no! Stay away from him. That fellow has a reputation of being the biggest art faker west of Moscow!"

Chris's face was grim as he returned to the cab.

"What's the word?" Geronimo queried.

"Not good. I'm afraid the enemy scouts have spotted our smoke. He says Valaud is the chief Red agent in this neck of the woods!"

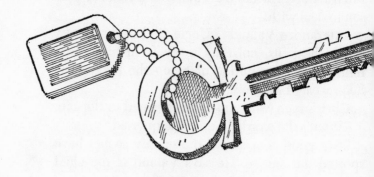

7 · The Omega Key

GERONIMO GRUMBLED AS their taxi started up again. "Things are really getting muddied up at the water hole. First TOAD—then the Chiller. Now this Valaud horns in and it turns out *he* makes medicine for the Reds."

The taxi finally pulled up at Triquet's lodging house. When Chris asked to come in and talk some more about Anson, Brigitte agreed.

As she fumbled in her bag for a key, Chris remarked, "This door wasn't locked when I called here before. How come?"

Brigitte shrugged. "The concierge must have returned. I know her—she is an old gossip. Often she goes out to chat and leaves it open."

"Let's ask her about this afternoon."

"*Eh bien.* There she is now."

The concierge—a jolly-looking woman with a triple chin and wearing a tent-sized red dress—was peering at them from her room. She proved eager to talk.

Mais oui, she had gone out. Sometime after four o'clock, it was, to visit a sick friend down the street. That was the only time all afternoon. True, she had not locked the door because she had not expected to stay away long.

"Why do you ask, mademoiselle?" she went on, darting curious glances at the two Americans. "Did anything happen? Besides that explosion, I mean! You heard it, of course. Like an atomic bomb. At first I thought the Germans were attacking Paris again!"

Brigitte managed to evade her questions and they started upstairs.

"Well, Gerry, you were right," Chris said. "That explains why the ice hadn't been outside the door long when I arrived. Probably the Algerian couldn't slip in to plant it till after she left."

On the top floor they walked down the grimy hallway to Triquet's studio. Brigitte stopped short in surprise.

The letters "CA" had been scratched in the wood of the door, as if with a knifepoint!

Chris looked at Geronimo, both thinking the same thing. CA—*Ciel Assassin!* . . . Skykill, the secret weapon Anson had been trying to track down when he ran afoul of the Chiller!

"What does it mean? Have you any idea?" Chris asked Brigitte.

Her face had taken on a puzzled, frightened look. "I—I do not know." Raising her voice, she shouted, "Paul! . . . Paul, *tu es là?*"

There was no answer.

Brigitte tried the door. The knob turned readily, and the boys followed her inside.

Triquet lay sprawled on the floor!

With a cry of fear, Brigitte ran to him. Chris and Geronimo examined the artist.

"Is he . . . dead?" she faltered.

"Unconscious," Chris said. "From the look of that bruise on his temple, he was knocked out."

The studio had been ransacked. Chris and Geronimo soon revived Triquet and helped him to a chair. The artist was dazed but able to talk.

"*Mon Dieu!* What happened, Paul?" Brigitte asked, wringing her hands nervously.

"I got slugged," said Triquet, fingering his swollen temple. "No doubt it shows well enough, eh?"

"But how? Who did it?" Brigitte was already getting a cold, wet towel for the bruise.

Triquet shrugged angrily. "I did not even see. It was soon after you left with—with—" He gestured toward Chris.

"My name is Cool—Chris Cool," said the blond TEEN agent. "And this is my friend, Geronimo Johnson."

Triquet eyed the Apache's copper complexion and long black hair. "American also?"

"Original settler," Geronimo said.

"Ah, *je comprends.* . . . Anyhow, as I was saying, it was soon after Brigitte and Monsieur Cool left here—maybe five, ten minutes. Suddenly I heard a scratching noise at the door. Well, I am no fool, you understand—not after I have nearly been bombed! So I tiptoe over and listen. The scratching ceases. But someone *must* be out there. Then I pull the door open fast."

Triquet snorted in disgust. "No one in sight. So I stick my head out to look down the hall. *Wham!* Someone hits me very hard. That is all I remember."

Chris glanced at Brigitte. "Did you have anything valuable around here?"

Triquet cut in. *"Mais certainement!* My paintings!" He waved at the canvases scattered about the studio.

"I meant anything of Anson's that your cousin may have brought when she came here?"

Brigitte gasped and hurried across the room to the curtained-off living space. A few moments later she reappeared.

"Oui! Something has been taken."

"What was it?" Chris asked.

"A key."

"To what?"

Brigitte sank down on a couch. "I think I had

better tell you everything. . . . Does the word
'Omega' mean anything to you?"

"Sure. It was a code name Anson used."

"*Oui*—and also a letter in the Greek alphabet.
The symbol for it was stamped on the key."

Brigitte paused as her voice choked. "You know
all about him, I suppose, Monsieur Cool. But at
first I knew nothing of Ivor's work. Only later,
when he was in fear of his life, did he reveal that
he was a secret agent."

Chris nodded. "What was the key for?"

"A sort of mailbox, at a cheap jewelry shop."
Brigitte named an address in a poor section of
Paris near the Gare St. Lazare railroad station.
"Ivor had many contacts in the underworld," she
went on, "and sometimes he bought information
from criminals or from double agents—people
working for the other side. But he had to guard
his real identity, you see, so he used the store as a
letter drop for messages—always under this code
name 'Omega.'"

"Was the setup still in use—even after he left
Paris?"

"I do not know. But earlier Ivor had received a
tip there about some very important information
he was after."

"About—Skykill? *Ciel Assassin?*"

Brigitte shrugged blankly. "He did not tell
me—only that the information was terribly important and urgent. And that someone was willing to

sell him this information for fifty thousand dollars."

The lead that Q had mentioned! Chris felt a mounting thrill of excitement. "Exactly how did Anson get this tip?" he pursued.

"A message was left at the store telling him to phone a certain number at a certain time. Something like that. Anyhow, a woman's voice answered. She was acting as go-between. She made the offer and Ivor agreed to her price."

"What were the arrangements?"

"He was to meet the person who had the information at a town called Brécy. Every year a festival is held there. It begins on the night of April twenty-seventh with a fete—a big open-house party—at the castle of the Count de Brécy. Many people come and it is not difficult to obtain an invitation."

Chris said, "And Anson was to make contact with this unknown person at the party?"

"Yes. But the meeting would be very risky and dangerous to both of them if it was found out. So they had to plan the details with great care."

"How were they supposed to identify each other?"

"The person was to have an X painted on the back of his left hand in invisible dye. I think Ivor was the one who insisted on this. He himself was to carry a device that gave off ultraviolet light—and its rays would make the X mark visible."

Chris and Geronimo traded glances. Both guessed at once that Anson had planned to wear a UV ring—a top-secret device used by CIA agents for identification and code purposes.

Geronimo shook his head dubiously. "Sounds like a ticklish job. He might have had to check out most of the people at the party—and do it all without attracting attention."

"Perhaps so . . . what does it matter?" Brigitte's shoulders drooped unhappily. "Before Ivor could go to Brécy, the Chiller closed in on him. Three times Ivor was almost killed in fiendish 'accidents.' Every move he made seemed to be watched. He did not even dare contact your Intelligence people in Paris. But in the end, *Le Glacier* got him, even in America. Just as he will get us, too!"

Triquet sprang up, clutching his mop of hair dramatically. "I have had enough of this business. I do not intend to get myself rubbed out—even for you, my dear cousin! Why do we not go to the police?"

"You think they could save us from *Le Glacier*?" Brigitte said scornfully.

Chris paced back and forth for a few moments. Then he turned to the girl and the artist. "Have you two any money? Enough to get out of Paris and lie low somewhere?"

Brigitte hesitated. "I have a little left. Perhaps if Paul could sell another picture—"

"There's no time for that," Chris said brusquely. He peeled several bills from his wallet and pressed them into her hand. "Is there a back door to this building?"

"*Oui.*"

"Then clear out tonight. Get as far from Paris as you can. And drop me a line care of American Express to let me know where you are."

Cutting short their fervent thanks, Chris left with Geronimo through a rear alley. On the nearest boulevard the boys caught a taxi, watching out the rear window to make sure they were not being followed.

Finally Geronimo settled back. "As they say in the comic books, the plot thickens—eh, *choonday?*"

"If it gets any thicker, we'll be swimming in glue."

"You realize the Chiller could be out to get us next?"

Chris nodded thoughtfully. The fact that the Citroen parked near the Eiffel Tower disappeared worries me. Whoever took it may have us spotted but good!"

"So what do we do now?"

"Keep Anson's date, naturally. Go to Brécy and find the man with the X on his hand."

"That's what I thought." Geronimo grunted. "Ask a foolish question, get a foolish answer!"

8 · Green Smoke

"No REASON WHY I can't take Anson's place," said Chris. "The fete at Brécy will be on April twenty-seventh—Thursday night. That gives us three days to set things up."

"You'll pose as Omega and contact X?"

"Sure, why not? If he's willing to sell the information on Skykill for fifty grand, he's not going to quibble over who pays. After all, he doesn't know Omega's real identity."

"We hope," Geronimo corrected dryly.

Chris frowned. "You think someone betrayed Anson?"

"It figures, doesn't it? How else did the Chiller get on his trail?"

"All that may have nothing to do with Skykill," Chris argued. "But let's say you're right. Where did the leak occur?"

"Maybe from the go-between—the woman he talked to on the phone."

Chris looked doubtful. "Like a lot of other people, she knew someone named Omega was in the market for information, and would pay for it. But she didn't know who Omega was. Seems more likely the jewelry-shop owner sold him out."

"Could be," the Apache conceded. "Which brings up another point. What about this stolen key?"

"Good question. If there's any message in Omega's drop box, we'd better lay hands on it before someone else does."

Chris gave the address of the jewelry shop to their driver. Both boys were silent as their taxi rolled along through the gathering darkness. Street lamps had been turned on and store signs flashed brilliantly along the boulevards.

In the dingy neighborhood behind the Gare St. Lazare, the taxi pulled to a stop. The street was shrouded in gloom except for a few lights here and there, mostly from upper windows.

The driver gave the boys a curious glance as Chris paid him off. "Shall I wait, monsieur?"

"*Non. Merci.*"

The jewelry shop was closed for the night, with

an iron grille pulled across the front. Its display window was crammed with gaudy, cheap-looking necklaces and rings.

Geronimo peered at the windows above the shop. All were dark. No one answered when Chris tried the bell at the doorway leading to the upper-floor apartments.

"Nobody home," said Geronimo. He looked at Chris, then away, and began humming one of his Apache war chants.

"The owner may live in back," said Chris. "Let's check."

The boys skirted around the block. At the rear ran a narrow alley. They counted off the individual buildings until they came to the one which housed the jewelry shop. It had a single window on the ground floor, also dark. But the back door was slightly ajar!

"Well, well," Geronimo murmured. "Maybe we're too late."

"Think we should—"

"Sh! Be as silent as an Indian."

The boys strained their ears for several minutes but could hear nothing. Finally Chris reached out to push the door open.

"Hold it!" Geronimo's scalp prickled with a sudden sense of danger. "Let's not go walking into anything, *choonday*."

"You're right. Stand clear, Gerry."

As Geronimo moved aside, Chris flattened himself against the wall and nudged the door with his toe.

Blam! With a loud report and a blinding flash, a white sheet of flame spat from the doorway! The flame fizzled out into a cloud of green, luminous smoke. It was acrid and nauseating.

Chris ripped open his tie and molded the special material over his nose and lips to form a TEEN agent's emergency gas mask.

The smoke was growing thicker and billowing through the whole alley. Roused by the blast, the neighborhood had suddenly come alive. Windows were flung open or slammed shut. Voices were shouting. A policeman's whistle shrilled.

Chris clenched his eyes against the stinging gas and groped blindly for Geronimo. Instead, his hand bumped something that felt like the snout of a gas mask. He clawed at it, trying to grapple with the wearer.

But a fist slammed him aside and a cold knife blade grazed his cheek. Whoever had been inside the shop was getting away!

Suddenly a friendly hand gripped his arm. Geronimo! Together they fled down the passageway. In a few minutes the pair slowed glumly to a walk on a nearby boulevard.

"Let's look at it this way," said Geronimo. "That gas probably did a great job of exterminating all the rats in the alley."

"Not quite," Chris said sourly. "The biggest one

got away. Whoever stole the key set that booby trap on purpose, in case we came and interrupted him."

They stopped at a café while Chris phoned the CIA station chief. "Wunny again, Uncle Phil. I know this is short notice but we're eager to see you."

"Tonight? . . . Dear me, I'm sorry, my boy, but I'm about to retire in—oh, forty minutes."

Chris glanced at his watch. 8:21. "Too bad. However, we couldn't have made it before nine-thirty, anyhow. Some other time, then. . . . How are you and Aunt Maud looking these days?"

"Oh fine, fine. She had her hair tinted today— lovely shade, like maples in October. *Très gai.* Been suffering a slight cold, myself. Have to wear a cloak when I go out."

"Very sensible. Where could I get one?"

"Try a tailor over on the Left Bank. He's Scotch, oddly enough. Name's Campbell—Lee Campbell. Has a small cellar shop."

Chris hung up and turned to Geronimo. "All set."

"Where do we meet him?"

"Must be one of those cellar night clubs on the Left Bank—what they call a *cave.* We'll have to check out the name first."

After reclaiming Geronimo's bag from his rented room, the boys went to their hotel to clean up. Checking through a tourist directory in the

lobby, they found a night spot listed by the name
of Le Cannibale.

"That's it," said Chris. "He'll be wearing a cloak
and she has reddish-dyed hair."

The place was a smoky, stone cellar decorated
with modernistic paintings. The waiters who
dodged among the tables were made up like can-
nibals, in black fuzzy wigs with white plastic
bones clipped to their noses. Couples were dancing to the music of a Negro jazz combo.

"Listen to that right hand on piano," said Chris.
"Very good. Like filigree!"

Geronimo pointed to the hamburger he was
trying to eat. "Very bad. Like mule meat."

"It's all they serve here. Guess I should've told
Uncle Phil we hadn't eaten yet."

"Great. We come to Paris and eat hamburgers.
I should have stayed on the reservation."

A few minutes after nine-thirty a small, dumpy
baldheaded man in a velvet cape came sweeping
into the room. A huge, muscular woman with or-
ange-red hair clung to his arm.

"*Ai!*" Geronimo gasped, choking on a bite of
hamburger. "Don't tell me this is Uncle Phil and
Aunt Maud!"

"His real name's Grubb," Chris muttered under
his breath. "Q says he poses as a nutty poet for
cover. The woman's his secretary and bodyguard."

The couple drew scarcely a glance from the

odd types at the night club. Chris and Geronimo stood up to greet them. The man flung back his cloak and peeled off gloves to shake hands.

"My dear chaps, how are you?"

Chris pulled out a chair for the woman. Her massive arms and shoulders looked powerful enough for a pro tackle. She wore a fixed smile.

Grubb leaned toward the boys. "Aunt Maud's deaf and can't speak. But believe me, not dumb. She can read lips in five languages and murder you at karate."

Geronimo stared at her admiringly. "That's what I call a real squaw."

"Quite right, my boy. She's worth her weight in gold, and that adds up to a sizable bit of bullion."

The CIA man said he had tipped off French Intelligence that the three thugs on the Eiffel Tower were enemy agents. "They're all safe in the clutches of the Deuxième Bureau, but so far there's no report on that Citroen."

Chris related their own adventures. Grubb pursed his lips thoughtfully on hearing Chris's plan to keep Anson's rendezvous at Brécy.

"Fifty thousand, eh? Lot of money, my boy. Still it may be worth the gamble, if we can squeeze that much out of the home office. Now then, about Brécy. I've heard of this annual shin-dig the count throws at his chateau. Quite an affair, they say. Shouldn't be too hard to get in, but you'll need cover. . . . Hm!"

Grubb twiddled his thumbs in thought. The woman tapped his arm and made rapid signs with her fingers.

"Ah, yes. Very clever of you, my dear. She's reminding me there's a girl's finishing school down there. That could be a useful angle."

The CIA man promised to transmit a coded message to New York immediately and to get in touch with the boys as soon as he had news.

Chris and Geronimo slept late the next morning. With their French windows wide open to the sunshine, they discussed their plans for the day over croissants and chocolate.

"What about the jewelry shop?" said Geronimo. "Think we could get anything out of the owner?"

"No harm in trying. At least we might find out if Omega's mailbox got cracked last night."

On their way out through the lobby, the boys passed a girl talking on one of the house phones. Chris froze and plucked Geronimo's sleeve. "That girl! I just heard her say *Skykill!*"

Geronimo veered to a table in the lobby and pretended to leaf through some travel folders while he looked her over. She was young and dressed in a pink spring outfit.

"Looks American to me," Geronimo commented.

Chris gave a slight nod. "Just a tourist, maybe. But we'd better find out."

"You want to rope this filly by yourself?"

"Might be easier. Why don't you tool along to that jewelry shop and check back later?"

Geronimo strolled off and went out the front door of the hotel.

Chris studied a folder describing the sights of Paris until he saw the girl hang up the phone. Then he walked over and spoke to her.

"Excuse me, but aren't you a Cliffy?"

The girl giggled nervously, displaying buck teeth. She had stringy, mouse-colored hair and was wearing fancy sunglasses. "Me? From Radcliffe? Gosh, no. Just Mid-State Teachers College. But I suppose I ought to be flattered—or should I?"

"Depends on what you think of Cliffies," said Chris, giving her his most Ivy League smile. "In your case, no flattery is necessary. I just thought I remembered seeing you up there."

Her name turned out to be Veronica Schlumbacher. Chris felt a twinge of doubt, which sharpened later over lunch at the Closerie des Lilas. With her sunglasses off, she looked even worse. Chris wished she had left them on. Bit by bit, he worked the conversation around to ask whom she had been talking to in the lobby.

"Oh, that was Tina Foss, the girl I'm traveling with. She called just as I was going out so I took it on the house phone." Veronica giggled again.

"She told me she'd just met a boy from her home town—Schuylkill, Pennsylvania."

Chris groaned inwardly. The girl had said "Skōol-kĭl," not Skykill. Why hadn't he listened more carefully! Now he might be stuck with this female the rest of the day.

After dessert Chris excused himself to make a phone call, saying he had to check with his roommate. "We—er—have an appointment at two o'clock. Probably tie us up for dinner."

Veronica looked disappointed as Chris hurried off. The hotel switchboard operator told him there was no message from Geronimo but that she would try their room.

He heard two rings. Then the phone was lifted. "*Allô?*"

Chris's pulse skidded. Whoever had answered was certainly not Geronimo! Disguising his voice, he said in French, "Is this room 412?"

"*Oui.*"

"Monsieur Cool, please."

There was a moment's pause before the voice replied. "This is Monsieur Cool speaking."

9 · The Sleeping Turk

CHRIS FELT A weird sense of unreality, hearing another person claim to be himself. The effect was distinctly unpleasant. Someone was not only on his trail, but that "somebody" was in his room at that very moment, no doubt exploring his and Geronimo's luggage!

"Who is calling, please?" the voice demanded sharply.

Chris thought fast and replied, "My name is— shall we say, *Ciel Azur,* to be discreet?" The answer would reveal whether his unknown visitor knew anything of *Ciel Assassin.*

"Ah, *oui*"—there was a hissing intake of breath—"I understand."

Might as well make the bait as big as possible

and try to hold him there, Chris decided. "I have the information you want," he went on. "I must deliver it to your hotel at once."

The voice at the other end tried to stall. "I—I was just about to leave, monsieur. It would be much more convenient if we could meet later, somewhere else."

"Impossible!" Chris snapped. "If you want the information, Monsieur Cool, you had better stay there and wait for me!"

He hung up the phone before the man could object.

Returning to their table on the terrace, Chris apologized to Veronica. "What a break!" he grumbled. "I was hoping we might see the Louvre together this afternoon, but I guess that's out. The appointment's all set for two o'clock."

Veronica was staring down sadly at her plate. "Of course. Th-that's quite all right," she gulped.

"It's an interview for a job at one of those youth hostels," Chris fibbed uncomfortably. "We may have to leave Paris tomorrow, so I—er—probably won't see you again."

Veronica said that she understood and put on her sunglasses hastily. Chris felt more like a heel than ever.

"May I drop you anywhere?"

"No, thanks. I—I may do a bit of window-shopping. That's what I was planning before we met. Thank you ever so much for the lunch."

Chris taxied back to the Hotel L'Empereur alone. At the reception desk in the lobby, he paused to check on their room key.

It was gone from its hook.

"There are two of you in 412, are there not, monsieur?" said the clerk. "No doubt it was your companion who took it."

"How long ago did he get back?" Chris probed.

The clerk gave a Gallic shrug. "I could not say, monsieur. I came on duty only two or three minutes ago."

Chris took a self-service elevator up to the fourth floor, his brain working rapidly. If Geronimo had returned and walked in on their unexpected caller, anything might have happened.

On the other hand, the phony "Monsieur Cool" might have filched the key himself when the concierge was not looking.

Before stepping out of the cage, Chris twirled the stem of his wrist-watch communicator to Transmit position, then pulled the stem outward. If Geronimo was anywhere within a range of several miles, he would hear a sharp buzz.

There was no response. Chris signaled again. Still no answer. So "Monsieur Cool" must be the one who had taken the key!

Mentally Chris debated the best strategy. Getting into the room without a key was no problem—the TEEN agents' training course had fully prepared him to cope with any type of lock. But how to catch the visitor off guard?

"The French windows!" Chris thought. The outer balcony, he recalled, ran all along the side of the building. If he could slip through one of the adjoining rooms, then he could approach their own room from the balcony—perhaps even observe "Monsieur Cool's" activities unaware. Chris tiptoed softly along the carpeted corridor. The second room before 412 bore a Do Not Disturb sign in French, hanging from the doorknob. He put his ear close to the panel. Loud snores vibrated the woodwork.

Chris lifted the sign gently from the knob. It was plastic—excellent for his purpose. He inserted the sign in the crack of the door and expertly "loided" back the tongue of the lock.

The hinge creaked slightly as he opened the door. Chris froze, but the snores continued. With his pulse thudding only twenty beats per minute faster, he closed the door behind him.

The room was in deep shadow, with the curtains drawn across the French windows. A huge, bull-like man was lying asleep on the bed in his underwear. His head was shaven egg-smooth and a large black handle-bar mustache branched out luxuriantly under his hooked nose. His mouth was hanging open and the mustache quivered delicately on the exhaust-stroke of each snore.

Holding his breath, Chris tiptoed across the room. He had nearly made it to the window when—*crash!* In the semidarkness he had knocked over a suitcase!

The snores ended with an explosive snort as the sleeper in the bed stirred. Chris barely had time to drop to a crouch behind an armchair, then the bedsprings creaked as the man sat upright.

He gave a deep baritone grunt and cleared his throat with a noise like boulders rumbling down a tin roof. Chris peered out cautiously and saw him hulked on the edge of the bed, yawning and scratching himself awake.

"How do I get out of this one?" Chris thought nervously.

Presently the man got up, stalked over to the windows, and drew the curtains aside. The action was alarming in more ways than one. The fellow was much bigger than he had appeared while horizontal—at least six-feet-six—and was mus-cled like Mr. America. The shaven head, hawk nose, and fierce mustachios made him look like one of those professional wrestlers who like to bill themselves under some such name as the Turkish Strangler.

Chris began to perspire freely.

The man opened the windows and breathed in deep gusts of fresh air. Chris estimated his chest measurement as somewhere around forty-nine or fifty inches exhaled, and his collar size as eighteen or nineteen at the smallest.

The TEEN agent literally stopped breathing in fear that the man might glance behind the chair at any moment. Instead, he turned away, walked across the room, and began rummaging on the floor of the closet.

"Now what?" Chris wondered.

The answer came as the man straightened up, clutching a pair of enormous dumbbells. For the next five minutes he went through a vigorous exercise routine, twirling the dumbbells as easily as if they were baby rattles.

Cold sweat trickled down Chris's skin. He caught several fleeting but terrifying glimpses of the fellow's biceps bulging like pumpkins.

Chris was numb with cramp and prolonged anxiety when the Terrible Turk finally put away the dumbbells. He stalked into the bathroom and closed the door. Soon after came the hissing noise of the shower.

For a moment Chris closed his eyes in relief and mopped the beads of perspiration from his forehead. Then, painfully, he arose from his crouch and hobbled toward the windows. One leg almost crumpled under him, but he rubbed away the pins and needles and made it safely to the balcony.

Outside, he moved swiftly along the balcony to

his own room and peered in. To his surprise, it appeared empty!

Was he too late? Had the intruder left without waiting for "Ciel Azur"? Or was he still lurking about?

Chris watched for a minute or two, uncertain what to do next. Slowly, cautiously he eased the French windows open and stepped inside.

Then the roof caved in as someone nailed him with a karate chop to the back of the neck!

10 · Bug Trouble

CHRIS DROPPED TO his knees with shooting stars of pain lancing through his skull and oscillating up and down his spinal column. For an instant he poised on all fours, trying to gather his wits.

Then a hand clutched the back of his coat to yank him upward.

Chris grabbed his assailant's wrist and flung him head over heels through the air. As the fellow landed on his back with a thud, Chris pounced like a tiger.

"I surrender! . . . From where the sun now stands, I shall fight no more!"

The red mist cleared from Chris's eyes to reveal the face of Kingston Two goggling up at him.

"Geronimo!" Chris released his grip hastily.

The Apache got to his feet, still looking a bit pop-eyed. He had a towel knotted around his waist and his lank black hair was wet, as if he had just stepped from the shower.

"Look, *choonday*," he grumbled. "I know I didn't greet you very nicely as you came in, but did you have to throttle me like that? I was only trying to pick you up and apologize."

Chris grinned wryly. "Apologize? Listen, you just about decapitated me with that karate chop."

"So—a slight mistake. Anyhow, what's the idea of sneaking in through the window? Don't you know that's dangerous with an Indian in the house? It makes me nervous."

Chris sank into an armchair, rubbing the back of his neck. "I was expecting to find someone else in here." He told about the phone call from the restaurant and his ruse to bait the intruder.

"Must have been the same person I cut sign on," said Geronimo.

"You spotted him?" Chris asked eagerly.

The Apache shook his head. "No, but I knew somebody had been here searching our gear—and not too long ago. The toothpaste was squeezed out, and someone had been prying at the fittings on our suitcases. There were still drops of water in the sink that hadn't dried yet, where he washed the toothpaste down the drain."

"Apparently my bait didn't tempt him," Chris reflected with a frown.

"Don't be too sure," said Geronimo. "I have a hunch he was still around and ducked out a window when he heard my key in the lock. That was probably right after you called."

"Why didn't you answer my buzz on the walkie-talkie?"

"Didn't hear it." Geronimo held out a bare left wrist. "I took off my watch before I climbed into the shower. I was just toweling off when you came pussyfooting around."

Chris got up from his chair to examine the suitcases. "Anything missing?" he inquired.

"Not as far as I can tell. But neither of us was carrying anything except our personal gear. Unless he came here to . . ."

Geronimo's voice trailed off. The two TEEN agents looked at each other suddenly as the same thought occurred to both.

Chris drew his wallet from a hip pocket and plucked out a wafer of plastic that looked like an ordinary credit card. He moved about the room, holding it close to the walls and furniture. When he came to the telephone on the night table, the raised lettering on the card suddenly glowed red.

"How do you like that for a dirty trick?" said Geronimo. "The guy comes to pay us a nice social call and bugs our telephone."

Chris unscrewed the base plate of the phone cradle. A small block of crystal-clear plastic had been clamped inside. It contained a cluster of tiny solid-state electronic components. Chris yanked the device out to examine it.

Geronimo gave a low whistle. "That guy knew his business!"

Chris nodded. The bug was designed to respond to a single note of the scale. Whoever planted it had only to call from his own telephone and then, while the call was ringing, sound the note on a mouth organ or tuning fork.

After that—even though the bugged telephone was not answered or lifted from its hook—he could eavesdrop on anything said in the room or on any future phone conversation.

"This circuitry looks as if it was made in one of the Red countries," Chris murmured.

"Valaud!"

"I'd bet on it. Wonder how he tracked me down to this hotel."

Geronimo shrugged. "At least we're onto him, too."

Chris slipped the bug into his pocket to send to Pomeroy for technical analysis. "How'd you make out at the jewelry shop?" he asked.

"Heap bad medicine! The place was crawling with police. It looked as if they were taking the whole shop apart, piece by piece."

"What about the owner?"

"Ah, now we come to the interesting angle," said Geronimo. "The guy has disappeared."

"How'd you find out?"

"Easy. Everybody on the block was talking about him. His name is Julius Hoche. He hasn't been seen since last week, and his shop has been locked and barred ever since—until today."

Chris gave his partner a worried look. "That could explain how Anson got rumbled. Maybe this Hoche didn't sell him out after all. Maybe Hoche himself was kidnapped and worked over till they pried Anson's name out of him."

Geronimo nodded. "You may have something there. What's the dope on that girl?"

"False alarm. Her name is Veronica Schlumbacher—she's from Mid-State Teachers College —and she was talking about Schuylkill, Pennsylvania, not Skykill. It cost me an hour and a half of small talk and an expensive lunch to find out."

Geronimo started to grin, then his face hardened. "Wait a second. You sure she wasn't giving you the old double shuffle?"

"How so?"

"She says Schuylkill *now*. But maybe it's no coincidence that Red joker was casing our room while you were buying her lunch."

Chris chewed on the idea for a moment. "You mean she dropped that word 'Skykill' on purpose just to hook our attention?"

"Why not? She may have been hanging around the lobby just waiting to snaffle us."

"Why bother? We were going out, anyhow."

"Sure," said Geronimo, "but we might have

been back five minutes later for all he knew. Maybe the guy wanted time to give our room a real going-over—so her job was to keep us occupied."

Chris frowned doubtfully. "If this gal was just acting, she could draw raves on Broadway. . . . Still, maybe we ought to check her out."

He picked up the phone and called the desk. "Is a young lady named Mademoiselle Veronica Schlumbacher registered at the hotel?"

"*Oui*, monsieur. Room 307."

Chris hung up. "Well, that proves part of her story."

"It doesn't prove she's not a phony."

"With a name like that? From Mid-State Teachers? The Reds aren't that clever!"

Geronimo began toying with a black obsidian knife that he had brought east with him from the Mescalero Apache Agency.

"There's one way to find out for sure," he said casually.

"Forget it. We can't go breaking into her room."

"Think she's back yet?"

"Well, no. She said she was going to do some window-shopping, but—"

"What about a roommate?"

"Some girl named Tina Foss. She's the one who's out with a guy from Schuylkill."

"Fine. Then the coast is clear."

"But listen—"

"Relax, *choonday*." Geronimo patted Chris soothingly. "We're both Ivy League gentleman-spies. Heaven forbid that we should stoop to any sordid breaking and entering. Just a little small-scale bugging of our own should do the trick."

Geronimo dressed and the boys descended to the third floor. They listened carefully outside 307 but could hear nothing. Then the Apache kept a sharp-eyed lookout along the corridor while Chris knelt down at the door.

The electronic pickup looked like a tiny screw head. It had a magnetic base. Chris was positioning it close to the keyhole when he heard steps on the carpet inside—a fraction of a second too late.

The door opened before Chris could get off his knees. He found himself looking up into the startled face of Veronica Schlumbacher. His own face flushed a deep crimson.

"Why—Christopher Cool!" she exclaimed.

Chris scrambled awkwardly to his feet. "Hi, Veronica! I—er—I was just looking for my Phi Beta Kappa key."

"Oh, my goodness. Did you lose it?"

"Well—I—I *think* I did. I thought I heard it drop just as I was about to knock on your door."

He pretended to peer about the floor. As Veronica joined earnestly in the hunt, Chris decided it was high time to cut the comedy. "Never mind. I probably lost it up in my room somewhere," he told her. "I was hoping you'd got back. I wanted you to meet my roommate at Kingston—Geronimo Johnson."

Geronimo looked as impassive as ever. "How!" He raised one hand gravely in an Indian salute. "I'm a Mescalero Apache. It's our usual tribal greeting."

Veronica giggled. "Oh—isn't that *cute!*" Her face beamed with pleasure. "You must meet my roommate, Tina Foss! . . . But what about your appointment at two o'clock?"

"It was canceled," Chris said curtly.

"Goody! I'm so glad!"

Tina was already peering out at the boys. Veronica beckoned her to the door. She was also from Mid-State Teachers and very plump.

"Oh, what an exciting day!" she babbled. "First Ed Katz from Schuylkill and now we meet you two!"

Geronimo exchanged a wooden-Indian glance with Chris.

The four arranged to meet in the lounge off the lobby a few minutes later. On the way down Chris glared at Geronimo. "If there's one thing I can't stand it's a smart-alecky Indian," he muttered. "Next time you get me into a mess like this, there's going to be one fresh Apache scalp dangling from my belt."

"Ugh. White man speak with forked tongue."

Over cups of tea, dinner plans were discussed. Suddenly Chris heard himself being paged.

"Monsieur Cool? You have a phone call. You may take it on one of the house phones if you wish."

It proved to be Uncle Phil.

"Terribly sorry, my boy," he said, "but I'm afraid I shall have to call off our appointment. You know—the one with that Scotch cloak-and-suit salesman at nine o'clock."

"Quite all right, Uncle Phil. I understand perfectly. Things do come up all of a sudden."

"Exactly. I just received an urgent cable from overseas."

Chris walked cheerfully back to the lounge and broke the news that their job interview had just been rescheduled.

"Nine? Oh dear, what a shame!" wailed Tina. Then she brightened. "But that'll still leave us plenty of time for dinner!"

At twenty minutes to nine the boys dropped their dates at the hotel and went on to Le Cannibale. Uncle Phil and Aunt Maud were waiting at a corner table.

"Good news, *mes enfants*—the home office says A-OK on Brécy," he reported. "All systems go."

"What about the invitation to the fete?" Chris asked. "Also the money and the ring?"

"All taken care of. Apparently your chaps at

Luxury Motors have been busy little beavers while Paris sleeps. On Thursday morning you're to go to the girls' finishing school near Brécy. Ask for a young lady named Spice Carter. She'll have everything you need. Better go down by car. My private garage will fix you up with something nice and sporty. Now then, one final word."

"Yes, sir?" said Chris.

"If the contact is made successfully, you're to do everything in your power to keep Skykill out of enemy hands. Understand? Washington will go as high as a million or more—*if* you can make a deal for the device itself."

"And if not—?"

"Then your orders are to destroy it—regardless of personal risk." Grubb held a match to his cigar and drew on the flame with every sign of keen enjoyment. "Remember, this gadget could alter the balance of power in the cold war—and it seems the Pentagon takes a very dim view of that."

11 · Triple Choice

BRÉCY TURNED OUT to be a bustling little market town in the heart of the wine country of eastern France. Chris and Geronimo arrived there shortly before noon on Thursday.

Terraced vineyards covered the green slopes that ringed it. Overlooking the whole scene was the Chateau Brécy. Its cone-peaked towers and graceful gray-white stone walls loomed on a high riverbank just beyond the town.

The boys had driven down from Paris in a racy red Alfa-Romeo GTZ, provided by the CIA "garage." It was fully equipped for agent-assignment and had a souped-up 1,570 cc. Giulia engine that was tuned like a Swiss watch.

After registering at Brécy's only hotel, they inquired the way to the girls' finishing school.

"Ah, you mean Madame Avril's Lycée for young ladies?" He smiled jovially. "Take the east road out of town, messieurs. Look for the white mansion, about half a mile from Brécy."

In a few minutes the Alfa-Romeo was rolling up a graveled drive that swept past carefully manicured greensward to the porticoed entrance.

After pressing a bell, the boys were admitted to a lobby office. A severe-looking, elderly woman greeted them. She looked at the two American youths suspiciously.

"May I help you, messieurs?" Her tone implied that nothing would give her less pleasure.

"I'd like to see Mademoiselle Spice Carter," said Chris. "I believe she just enrolled here."

"*Oui.* Yesterday, to be precise. Your name, please?"

Presently a beautiful red-haired girl came tripping down a curved staircase into the lobby. One line of a nursery rhyme flashed through Chris's head: *Sugar and spice and all things nice . . .*

Then he remembered that red pepper was also a kind of spice. She looked as if she might have a pinch of that, too.

"Chris, darling!" She flitted across the parqueted floor and planted a breathless smack on his cheek. "How sweet of you to look me up! Of course you're going to take me to lunch?"

"Natch," said Chris. Close up, he noticed that she had emerald-green eyes.

Spice turned to Geronimo. "And who is this? Sitting Bull?"

"Sitting J. Bull to you, please," said the Indian with cold dignity.

She flashed him a dazzling smile and shook hands, giving the secret TEEN-agent grip. As the three made their way out of the lobby under the purse-lipped, disapproving gaze of the housemother, Geronimo muttered something to Chris.

"What language is that?" Spice asked. "Kickapoo?"

"Apache," said Chris. "He was just saying he thinks you must have been recruited from a school for backward girls."

"No, but he's close—Vassar."

Geronimo relented enough to grin.

"That's about as far as he ever goes," said Chris. "His name is really Geronimo Johnson and he has a weakness for red-haired squaws. He doesn't see too many on the reservation."

"I think he's smashing!" said Spice.

They squeezed into the Alfa-Romeo.

"About lunch," said Chris as they started down the drive. "Did you have any place in mind?"

"The girls recommended a hash house in town called Aux Trois Reines," Spice said. "Serves yummy snails."

"Snails it is." He headed back toward Brécy.

"By the way, just to clue you in, I'm supposed to be the daughter of a Texas oil millionaire. But it was said I was very unhappy at Vassar, so my alleged daddy at Luxury Motors made a transatlantic call Tuesday. He offered Madame Avril a piece of an oil well to let me enroll in mid-term. I just flew in from Paris yesterday."

Chris frowned. "I take it this setup has some connection with the party at Chateau Brécy tonight?"

"Right. Uncle Phil at the Paris station found out all the girls at the school are invited to the fete every year. You'll go as my date. So far I haven't found anyone for Geronimo but if he's with us, I'm sure he'll be admitted."

"What about the other items?" Chris inquired.

"Pull off the road for a minute."

From inside the lining of her spring raincoat Spice pulled out a wide zipper case of glove-soft leather. "There's fifty thousand dollars inside in used fifties."

Geronimo turned back the carpeting, pressed a button, and deposited the zipper case in a secret compartment under the floor.

Meanwhile, Spice had groped in her bag and brought out a man's white-gold ring, set with what looked like a sapphire. The ring did not form a complete circle but ended in two prongs. "Here's the UV gimmick. Know how it works?"

"Squeeze the prongs together?"

"Right. The stone is the ultraviolet lamp."

Chris examined the masterpiece of microcircuitry. He slipped it on his third finger and tested the action of the prongs.

"Be careful not to look straight at the stone," Spice warned. "You can't see the ultraviolet rays but they could ruin your eyes."

"What's the effective range?" Chris asked.

"About four feet. At that distance the rays fan out to cover a circular area four feet in diameter, so you should be able to check anyone's hand without too much fancy maneuvering."

In town, the cobbled streets and quaint old stone buildings were decked with gay flags and streamers for the annual spring festival. They soon found Aux Trois Reines—a medieval-looking restaurant nestled in the shadow of Brécy's Burgundian-Gothic-style church. Not far off stood a modern structure of chrome, steel, and glass.

Over lunch, Chris asked if Spice had found out anything about the fete or who would attend it.

"All sorts of people," said Spice. "Local society and the jet set from Paris and the Riviera. Quite a few foreigners too, from what the girls at the school say, including Americans. Seems the count gets around and has a wide acquaintance in diplomatic and artistic circles."

"Hm! Sounds like a full house."

After lunch the boys dropped Spice at the Lycée and spent the rest of the day prowling about the town and its environs to familiarize themselves with the terrain. Both thought it best not to be seen too close to the castle.

At eight o'clock, after changing into white dinner jackets, the boys called for Spice in the Alfa-Romeo. Cars were lined up on the drive to receive the girls and their escorts. Madame Avril, looking like a frigate in full sail, led the procession in an ancient but glossy Panhard.

Chateau Brécy was ablaze with lights. A pair of costumed footmen in knee breeches and powdered wigs checked the cars and their occupants. The line of automobiles crawled up the slope to the chateau, past a formal garden of topiary hedges and fruit trees, which were strung with glowing Japanese lanterns.

The chateau, half-stronghold and half-elegant country house, dated from the late Middle Ages. It was U-shaped, enclosing a front courtyard that faced the garden, with a spired, thick-walled tower at each corner.

Turning over their cars to attendants, the guests filed in through the wide open doors of the main hall. Under sparkling crystal chandeliers, they were greeted by the count.

"Nothing like this back on the reservation, eh Gerry?" Chris murmured.

"Oh, I don't know. You should see our medicine dance."

The Count de Brécy was a slim, elegant man of

fifty with a small, pointed beard and waxed mustache. Every now and then he waved his fingers and sniffed delicately at a perfumed silk handkerchief. His eyes lit up at sight of the red-haired Lycée student.

"*Charmante! Ravissante!*" he exclaimed, then took Spice's hand and kissed it resoundingly. "My dear, who dresses you?"

"Well . . . I do, really," said Spice.

"No, no, no!" The count fluttered his handkerchief. "Your clothes, I mean. That white gown. Where was it made? Who is your *couturier?*"

Spice's green eyes sparkled mischievously. "Oh, I just run up most of my things on the sewing machine."

The count giggled and patted her hand. "Naughty girl! You are pulling my leg now, mademoiselle, but I forgive you." He greeted Chris and Geronimo and turned to the couple behind them.

"Nothing like *that* back on the reservation," Geronimo muttered under his breath.

"He's not as sappy as he seems," said Spice. "Apparently he's done a lot for Brécy."

"Like for instance?" said Chris.

"Well, that modernistic building in town. It's an Agricultural Institute he endowed to help improve the local farm products."

A servant offered them glasses of punch from a tray. Chris was looking about, appalled at the number of people he would have to check.

"I'd better circulate around the garden," he re-marked in a low voice. "The fluorescent X mark may show up better in semidarkness."

The three strolled outdoors. Chris was startled as he recognized a figure standing near the punch bowl—a tall, gray-haired, mummy-like man in evening clothes.

Alexandre Valaud! He was with a younger man, dressed in a white jacket. Valaud's compan-ion was about twenty-five or thirty with a hard, deeply tanned Mediterranean type of face.

"The tall one's Valaud!" Chris whispered.

Geronimo's eyes narrowed. "Did they see us?"

"Don't know. Not yet, I think."

The TEEN agents veered wide of the large table loaded with platters of hors d'oeuvres, and wandered down the garden slope.

For the next half hour, Chris mingled with the throng, cautiously beaming his UV ring at every hand within range. He was beginning to grow slightly discouraged when suddenly he struck gold.

Under the ultraviolet rays, an X—pale green and luminous—glowed on the back of a man's left hand! He had rumpled sandy hair, an ill-fitting dark suit, and high Slavic cheekbones.

Chris drew a deep breath. He was about to release the prongs of the ring as a servant ap-proached with a tray of canapés.

The next instant Chris froze in disbelief. An X mark was showing on the servant's left hand!

Chris switched off the ring and the mark faded at once. He looked around, scanning the faces of other guests nearby. Apparently no one had noticed the briefly glowing symbols except his own two companions, Spice and Geronimo.

Chris exchanged glances with them. "You saw?"

Spice nodded. "Looks like double-stamp night."

They strolled off a few paces. "Two possible contacts!" Chris whispered.

"Which one has the phony?" said Spice.

"Why stop at two?" said Geronimo. "If someone's muscled into the act, there may be more."

"That's a cheery thought," Chris said. "But you're right. I'd better keep on checking. You two keep your eyes on this pair."

Moving on, Chris resumed scanning every knot of guests with his ring. Dinner was served, buffet style, but he stayed out of the food lines. By ten-fifteen he felt that he had checked everyone in sight except a man standing in the courtyard near the open doorway.

Chris moved closer to the man, squeezing the prongs of the ring to make it flash. His jaw tightened as a luminous X mark glowed on the left hand of Number Three!

12 · The Tower Room

THREE PEOPLE WEARING the invisible mark which
was to identify Omega's contact! There had certainly been a leak somewhere.

The third man, standing near the doorway of
the chateau, was middle-sized, compactly built,
with sharp, hard-bitten features. Chris's keen
eyes detected a suspicious bulge near the left
armpit of his tuxedo.

Of all three, he seemed the one best fitted for
the role of spy or double agent—a dealer in secret
information. Which proved nothing, Chris realized. The man's mission might well be to intercept Omega's contact.

Besides, there was the first man's Slavic facial

features. If not French, he might be a turncoat from behind the Iron Curtain with Red secrets to sell.

Then there was the second man, the servant. Who would be in a better position to eavesdrop on conversations or pick up valuable gossip? From what Spice had said, the count no doubt had a wide assortment of visitors at the chateau on whom the servant might have spied.

The man near the doorway had just handed his empty plate to a servant and was lighting a cigarette. Chris moved closer and spoke to him chattily in French.

"Quite an evening—eh, monsieur?"

The man's eyes, like steel needles, etched a slow portrait of Chris's face and filed it away. "*Une affaire formidable*," he agreed. "You are a friend of the count's?"

"Just a guest. A tourist, in fact."

"Ah. American?"

Chris nodded. "My name is Christopher Cool."

The man granted him a brusque handshake. "Fernac. I am a journalist from Paris."

"Here to report the party?"

Fernac shrugged. "Perhaps, if it is worth reporting. One sees celebrities—movie stars, diplomats. Sometimes their antics make news."

"What paper do you write for?" Chris asked, sounding avidly impressed. "*France-Soir?*"

"Free lance. . . . And you, Monsieur Cool, what do you do?"

Chris grinned sheepishly. "Just a college student. I came here with a girl from Madame Avril's Lycée, but I seem to have lost her somewhere."

Fernac turned away. "*C'est la vie.*" He seemed to have lost all interest.

Chris wandered off. A small stringed orchestra was playing under the Japanese lanterns and some of the guests were dancing. He caught sight of Spice, trapped among several of her schoolmates and their dates. Chris deftly extricated her and steered her out among the dancers.

"Any new candidates?" Spice inquired softly.

"One more. Tell you about him in a minute. . . . Think I see Geronimo over there. Let's go join him."

They danced clear of the other couples and strolled off toward the Apache, who was standing alone under a tree, nibbling a petit four.

Chris told about the third man with an X mark and pointed him out. "How about you two? Did you get a line on the others?"

Spice indicated the sandy-haired man with the high cheekbones. He was seated on a garden bench, sipping a glass of punch. "I wangled a short chat with him," she said. "He's an agricultural chemist doing research at the Institute in town. Name is Ravatsky. Came to France as a refugee, either from East Germany or Poland. He was a little vague about that."

"What about the other guy—the servant?"

Geronimo rolled his eyes. "On the right. With the coffeepot."

Chris glanced in the direction of the eye-roll. A colorful group which included several Africans in bright robes and an Indian prince were clustered around a French movie star. The servant, a stocky man with slick blond hair, was pouring demitasse for them.

"Find out anything about him?" Chris queried.

"Heard someone call him Moutin," said Geronimo. "I tried to palaver with him but he was too rushed to talk. I don't trust him. He's sly like a coyote."

"That figures, if he's an eavesdropper who peddles information," said Chris. "Might be the type who goes in for petty blackmail—only this time he stumbled on something big."

Geronimo nodded. "Could be."

"Which leaves us with the same problem," Spice murmured. "Which one is your real contact?"

Chris said slowly, "Anson knew the setup was dangerous. That probably means there are enemy agents on deck, watching the real X. If I identify myself to the wrong man, it could ruin our chances of getting the lowdown on Skykill."

"It could ruin you, *choonday*." The Apache's expressionless dark eyes met those of his partner.

Chris needed no warning. He was all too aware that he might be staking his life, once he made the contact. A wrong guess could be fatal.

"So what do we do?" asked Spice. She tried to make her voice sound as gay and casual as ever but did not quite succeed.

Chris pondered a moment. "Where's Valaud?"

The TEEN agents scanned the throng milling about the garden. The art dealer and his tough-looking companion were nowhere in sight.

"Maybe in the chateau somewhere," Spice said.

Chris went on thoughtfully, "The evening's not over yet. Let's keep an eye on all three X's and see if we can pick up a clue."

"Who'll watch whom?" Geronimo asked.

"Well, we've each spoken to one of them, so we'd better play it cool and switch. Geronimo, you keep tabs on Fernac. Spice, see what you can do with Moutin. I'll tail Ravatsky."

While Chris was speaking, the sandy-haired chemist rose from the garden bench and strolled toward the punch table. He set down his glass and stood gazing at the dancers.

Chris wandered off through the garden. Bit

by bit he worked his way toward the courtyard, where the punch table was located. Before he reached it, Ravatsky walked into the chateau.

Chris followed cautiously.

The great hall of Chateau Brécy was almost empty, except for servants going in and out. Several guests were admiring a huge tapestry that depicted a medieval hunting scene. Ravatsky was nowhere in sight.

Chris paused to get his bearings. A wall chart nearby, evidently for tourists on visiting days, bore a diagram of the chateau with labels in French, English, German, Spanish, and Italian. Chris pretended to study it.

Suddenly he stifled a gasp. The top room of one tower in the diagram bore a penciled X mark!

Was the mark simply a chance scrawl by a guide or visitor? Or had the real X put it there as a hint that Omega should meet him in that tower?

The chart was defaced with several scribbled initials and dates. The X mark might be just another scribble. Yet Chris had a strong hunch that it had been put there intentionally.

The tower with the mark was at the north rear corner of the chateau, overlooking the river. How to reach it? Chris studied the diagram more closely. The staircase from the main hall led to a gallery on the next floor. By following this gal-

lery to the right, he would reach a spiral staircase that wound upward into the tower.

But what if he were stopped by the count's
servants? Much worse, what if the enemy agents
had seen the mark! They might be lurking in the
chateau, on watch for anyone going to the tower!

"Better fake a disguise," Chris decided.

Several rooms opened off the great hall. Chris
sidled toward one that appeared dark and
slipped into it while no one was looking.

The room was furnished in Empire style. By
the light through the open doorway from the
brilliant chandeliers outside, Chris could see pur-
ple-and-gold-striped drapes shrouding the tall
windows. The TEEN agent grinned. "Just what
I need. A perfect set of threads for the well-
dressed Afro-Asian man-about-town!"

From the emergency kit strapped inside his
cummerbund, he took a small tin of dark ointment used for night commando operations and
a black nylon-elastic skullcap. Chris fitted the
cap tightly over his blond hair, then pushed up
his sleeves and rubbed the ointment over his face
and hands.

The stuff soon dried, staining his skin a dark
walnut hue. Tinted contact lenses over his blue
eyes completed the make-up job.

With a jackknife Chris slashed down one of
the drapes, mentally vowing to send the count
a payment for damages later. From part of the

material he fashioned himself a turban. The rest became a gaudy, poncho-style robe.

Emerging from the Empire room, Chris strode across the great hall and mounted the staircase. On the next floor he followed a long gallery—hung with portraits of De Brécy ancestors—to its end, where another corridor branched right, into the north wing. At the corner was a stone stairway spiraling up into the tower.

Chris began the long ascent. One floor up he encountered an ancient, gray-haired servant.

"Monsieur!" the old man quavered. *"Cette partie du chateau n'est pas ouverte au public!"*

Chris responded with a flash of white teeth and a cheerful flood of Swahili dialect. The old man looked confused, then shrugged and allowed the lordly looking African to pass.

Chris continued up the winding staircase. Here and there the curved stone wall of the tower was pierced with narrow windows. The diffuse glow of light from the lower floors gradually faded into enveloping darkness as he mounted higher and higher. Chris switched on his pocket flashlight but cautiously cupped its rays with his hands.

At last he reached the top. A massive wooden door blocked his way into the chamber. Chris hesitated, then flicked off his light and tried the antiquated bronze latch.

The door creaked open slowly. Inside was

darkness, broken only by faint shafts of moonlight filtering through two casement windows.

Chris closed the door cautiously behind him and switched on his flashlight again. The stone-flagged room was bare except for a large armoire, or wardrobe, and a long oak refectory table.

Now what? Simply wait for X to appear? Perhaps there was a message!

Chris strode across the room and opened the armoire. A dank smell of moldy wood greeted his nostrils. But the armoire was empty.

As he paused uncertainly Chris heard a faint sound of steps outside. Switching off his flashlight, he ducked softly into the wardrobe and pulled the door almost shut, leaving a crack just wide enough to peer through.

He crouched in the musty darkness, waiting. But whoever was outside the room made no move to enter. Instead, Chris heard a key turn.

He was being locked in the room!

A shrill peal of maniacal laughter echoed outside the chamber, making the short hairs bristle on Chris's scalp.

Utter silence followed. As he strained his ears to listen, Chris suddenly shivered. He had begun to feel chilly—his skin was tightening into goose bumps.

A terrifying thought pierced him. He pushed open the door and burst out. The whole room was growing colder! The temperature was dropping by the second!

Chris's heart lurched. It must have been the Chiller's crazy laugh that he had heard! He had blundered straight into a deadly trap!

13 · Fancy Footwork

CHRIS DARTED ACROSS the room and tugged at the door. Locked, as he had feared! And nothing short of a fire ax or battering ram could break through those heavy timbers!

He fought down a wave of panic. No use shouting for help because no one could hear him anyhow, so high up in the tower . . . except the Chiller!

"Turn blue, you creep!" he muttered.

Unfortunately he himself must be turning blue by now, Chris reflected. The temperature had fallen to at least zero. A fit of uncontrollable shivering seized him.

The windows! At least the air outside would be warmer than this stone-walled icebox!

108

Chris rushed to the nearest casement and fumbled at the latch with his numbed fingers. As the window swung open, he gulped greedily at the warmth of the April night. By comparison with the frigid chamber, it was like basking in front of a cozy fireplace. But the inside temperature was still plummeting.

Peering out the narrow window, Chris found that it faced away from the chateau. From the sill there was a sheer drop down the full length of the tower.

"The other window may overlook the main roof of the chateau," Chris thought.

He dashed to the other casement and yanked it open. Three or four feet below the window sill lay the steeply sloping chateau roof.

Chris hoisted himself up to the sill and thrust out one leg. This was going to be tricky—better not think about it too much. Clutching the sill for support, he squirmed out backward and withdrew his other leg.

Slowly, inch by inch, Chris eased himself downward, toeing the air for a foothold. A hissing sigh of relief escaped his lips as his right foot found the sloping surface of the roof.

Not a moment too soon! The door inside the chamber was creaking open. His enemy must have heard him going out the window—or was it enemies? The rush of footsteps sounded like more than one man.

Chris shrank back on one side of the window, flattening himself against the tower wall and clawing at its stone surface for support.

Presently a white-hooded figure craned low out of the open casement. The covered head turned to peer across the roof, displaying ghastly-looking eyeholes. Chris reached up and dealt a karate blow across the side of the man's neck. He slumped like a sack of flour. As he sagged, Chris's hand brushed scaly-slick crystals of ice from the surface of the hood.

Now he could see rays of light gleaming inside the chamber. So his hunch had been right! The hooded enemy was not alone! The unconscious man had fallen across the sill, head dangling. Slowly his white-clad form was pulled back into the room. Evidently his companion was dragging him out of the way to gain access to the narrow window.

Chris tensed himself breathlessly, his left hand groping inside his robe for the anesthetic pen, ready to zing off a sleepy sliver the instant a second man appeared at the window.

Instead, the light went out.

Chris breathed slowly and deeply, trying to keep calm. Agonizing moments dragged by and still nothing happened.

"He's going to wait me out," Chris realized.

The TEEN agent peered through the moonlit darkness. He was perched only a few feet from the edge of the steeply pitched slate roof. Beyond, except for a narrow stone gutter, there was nothing but empty air—and a sudden plunge if he lost his balance!

Chris began to perspire. What a spot to be in! And no way down but the tower chamber where his unseen enemy lay in wait.

If only he had worn his street shoes with the rocket-hopper soles! But his white dinner jacket called for patent leather pumps. No use crying about that now. His one hope was to figure some way out of his precarious position.

Again Chris peered around. Twenty feet away a dormer window protruded from the roof. If he could reach it, he might be able to open the window and squirm inside.

Getting there would be the problem. He would have to teeter his way along the edge of the roof—in full view of his enemy at the tower window! More minutes passed as Chris debated the odds. How much longer could he go on clinging to his present desperate spot? His nerves were wire-taut.

"I'll have to chance it," Chris decided.

Gripping his anesthetic pen, he lowered himself to a sprawling position on hands and knees. Cautiously he slithered downward until one foot came to rest in the trough of the stone gutter.

"Here's hoping it holds!" As Chris brought his other foot down, a roof slate suddenly came loose. It clattered off the roof and over the rim of the gutter with a noise that sounded to his ears like a mountain avalanche!

A white-hooded figure popped into sight at the tower window. Chris jerked up his anesthetic pen and took aim, but before he could press the clip, the man withdrew again.

Chris's heart was thumping, his breath coming in quick, nervous gasps. He closed his eyes for a moment to regain control of himself, then began inching his way, step by step, along the gutter toward the dormer window. His progress was agonizingly slow. He dared not think of the awful gulf of empty space behind and beneath him.

"Don't lose your cool, boy!" Chris muttered.

Beads of cold sweat were trickling down his face and chest. He was beginning to shiver again. Was it just the chill from his—

With a shock of fear, Chris realized the truth! His whole body was growing cold, his fingers were turning numb. The same thing was happening again as in the tower chamber! The same thing that had happened to Anson on the picnic ground at Funland!

Chris shot another glance at the tower window. The hooded figure could no longer be seen, but he was there, all right!

"I'll never make it," Chris realized. He was shivering too violently. The distance to the dormer window was too far. Soon his numbed fingers would no longer be able to clutch the roof for support.

He took a deep breath, steeling himself to glance downward, then turned his head and peered over his shoulder. Far below rippled the moon-silvered waters of the river. The steep cliff bank at the foot of the chateau was almost vertical, but not quite.

How deep was the water at this point? Could he clear the outcroppings of rock along the bank?

Balancing himself delicately against the roof, Chris shifted his right foot behind his left one, then turned slowly until he was facing outward.

Slowly he pushed himself upright. For a moment the TEEN agent poised on the edge of the gutter as he thrust his hands out in front of him. Then Chris flung himself through the air in a graceful swan dive.

His robe billowed like a flapping sail as he arced downward and outward from the chateau wall. Down—down—down!

Chris was hurtling at bullet speed as he hit the water with a mighty splash.

In the garden on the other side of the chateau, the splash went unheard, lost in the blaring music of the orchestra and the chatter of the party guests.

Meanwhile, Spice had been watching the servant Moutin. She had seen him pass between a double row of hedges, carrying a tray of empty plates, yet he failed to reappear at the other end of the row.

Puzzled, she went to look. The twin hedges formed a sort of enclosed alleyway leading up the hillside toward the chateau courtyard. The area was shadowed in darkness by the overhanging branches of trees. Moutin was nowhere in sight!

"He certainly didn't disappear into thin air!" Spice told herself angrily. She moved forward, up the slope, between the hedges. Suddenly she stopped short in the gloom. A strange glow was coming from the ground just ahead!

As Spice walked closer, she saw the source—a pitlike opening from which a short flight of three or four steps led down into the hillside.

"So that's where he disappeared!" Intrigued, the red-haired TEEN agent went down the steps. She was in a brick-walled tunnel, dimly lighted by a few naked bulbs. Presumably the tunnel led into the cellars of the chateau. "Must be a utility entrance for servants," Spice decided.

She walked slowly forward. Farther on, the passageway branched into three separate tunnels. Now what? Should she turn back and wait for Moutin to reappear?

Spice's feminine curiosity was aroused. "Eeny meeny miney moe," she whispered, then gave up the routine and decided to explore the right-hand branch.

The passage curved. Her steps echoed hollowly on the flagstoned floor. In a few moments she came to a stout wooden door. Spice tried the handle. The door was locked.

Had she made the wrong choice? Surely Moutin would not have bothered to lock it if the servants were using this route, to and fro, as they served the guests.

"On the other hand," Spice thought, "he may be up to something fishy!"

Groping in her evening bag, she took out a slender steel tool and deftly picked the lock in the approved fashion taught by the ex-safe-cracker who instructed all TEEN agents on locks, keys, and combinations.

The door opened on well-oiled hinges. Beyond lay pitch darkness. Spice stepped through the doorway, switching on her pocket flashlight.

"Yikes! What a perfect spot for ghouls!" she thought. She was in an ancient, vaulted stone cellar festooned with cobwebs.

A moment later Spice stiffened in horror. Those noises! Was she hearing things?

Her flesh crawled as they came again—queer jabbering, slavering noises, half human, half animal.

14 · Ask Me No Questions

CHRIS'S PLUNGE CARRIED him deep below the surface of the river. The robe hampered his movements and he doffed it clumsily underwater.

"Better not come up just yet," he thought. "Those white-hooded goons may be waiting to put the chill on me again!"

What was the secret of their fiendish trick? Anson had been iced quickly, in the space of a few moments. Chris had been luckier.

At first, while he was locked in the tower chamber, the Chiller's men had not known his exact position, so they were forced to chill the whole room, Chris reasoned. Only later, when the second thug had him clearly in sight on the roof, had the chill come on fast. This seemed to indicate that their gimmick, whatever it might be, could be aimed precisely.

Chris surfaced cautiously, showing only his head above water. He was out of the moonlit area, in the shadow of the chateau walls. It was difficult to make out much at the top of the tower, but he could see nothing that looked like a white hood at either window. Nevertheless, Chris submerged again and swam upriver a little distance from the chateau before coming ashore.

The bank was lower and gentler here, shadowed by drooping willows and shrubbery. Higher up the slope, huge ancient oak trees screened the glow of lanterns from the chateau garden.

Chris dragged himself out of the water, shivering in his wet clothes. "Great situation," he murmured wryly. "How do I explain this to my host and the other guests? Tell 'em I took a short moonlight dip in the fish pond?"

He twirled the stem of his wrist watch to Transmit position and gave it one pull. After several moments the voice of Geronimo responded in Apache:

"That you, *choonday?*"

Chris explained his plight. Geronimo listened and growled, "Why didn't you call me before?"

"So you could get iced, too?"

"Okay. Stay put. I'll see what I can do."

Chris scrubbed off what was left of the dark stain on his face and hands. Then he huddled in the shadows, waiting to hear from his partner. His heart did a flip-flop as a voice behind him suddenly barked:

"You're under arrest! No swimming allowed!"

"Gerry!" Chris went limp with relief as he made out the Apache's white-toothed grin in the leafy gloom. "What're you trying to do—give me heart failure?"

"Just testing. You'd better watch it, boy. In Apache country you'd be strung up by the heels over a slow fire by now!"

"Might not be a bad idea in these wet clothes. What have you got there?"

Geronimo hunkered down under the willows. "Something dry for you to put on."

Chris unrolled the bundle, which included a white dinner jacket, black evening trousers, shirt, tie, and cummerbund. "For Pete's sake, where'd you get these?"

"Ask me no questions, I'll tell you no lies. See how they fit."

Chris stripped off his sodden clothes and dressed hastily in the outfit which Geronimo had brought. The garments fitted fairly well, except that the pants were a bit loose.

As Chris transferred his waterproof emergency kit from his discarded wet cummerbund to the new one, he said, "Okay, now stop being so coy and tell me where all this came from."

"Well, if you must know, I left Valaud's pal back in the bushes in his skivvies."

Chris gave a low whistle. "Conscious?"

"Let's say his eyes were closed." Geronimo shrugged. "You know—a slight thumb squeeze at the proper pressure point below the ear."

"In the midst of a garden party?"

"Relax. Nobody sees an Apache who doesn't want to be seen. I waited till he was standing near some nice dark bushes."

"Great. And what happens when he comes to?"

"Look, white eyes," Geronimo said severely, "for a guy who just got water-cured, you ask a lot of questions. Valaud's a Red agent and his pal's in the same line of work, so let us not worry if their feelings get hurt. Wait'll I show you what I found in his pocket."

The Apache held up a small metal key, close to his flashlight. Chris's eyes widened. The key was stamped with the Greek letter Omega!

"Wow! So now we know who zapped Triquet and raided the jewelry shop! Anything else?"

"I left his wallet back in the bushes," said Geronimo. "His names's Barone. He was also carrying this news clipping."

Chris unfolded the clipping. It had been cut from a well-known French Communist news-paper and told how the President of the United

States would soon fly to Europe with a dozen top advisers for an important international conference.

"Hm! Interesting," said Chris. "I guess this settles which team he's on, all right. What I'd like to know is whether he and Valaud were the goons who tried to ice me in the tower."

"Could be," said Geronimo. "I spotted Baron coming out of the chateau right after you buzzed me for room service. Valaud was in the main hall admiring that big tapestry."

Chris frowned. "How about our three X's?"

Geronimo shook his head. "I doubt if any of them could have done it. I've been watching Fernac all along, and I saw Ravatsky out in the garden about five minutes before you called. Of course that still leaves Moutin, but I assume Spice has been watching him."

"Let's go find her," Chris suggested. "But first we'd better stash these wet clothes in the car."

The two youths made their way furtively to the parking area and deposited the bundled-up garments in the Alfa-Romeo. Then they returned to the garden. Spice was nowhere in sight.

"I'll call her," Chris said. In the shadow of a clump of trees, he signaled with two short buzzes on his wrist-watch communicator.

"Vassar One!" Spice's voice replied. She seemed to be speaking in an urgent whisper.

"Kingston One and Two. Where are you?"

"Some sort of cellar. It's creepy!" Spice hastily related how she had trailed Moutin through the hedge alley and into the underground tunnel entrance. "I came to three branching tunnels and took the right-hand—"

Her voice broke off suddenly in a stifled scream! Faint, confused noises followed.

"Come on!" Chris exclaimed. "She may be in trouble!"

"Over that way!" said Geronimo. "There's the hedge alley she spoke of!"

The boys made their way quickly among the garden-party guests and darted between the double row of hedges. They had just descended the stairs into the underground tunnel when Spice came running toward them. Her face was white with shock and fear.

"What happened?" Chris asked, taking her arm.

"Later!" Spice gasped. "Let's get out of here first!"

All three TEEN agents turned and hurried from the tunnel. Slowing their pace, they found a secluded garden bench and sat down. Spice was still panting.

"Okay, take it easy," said Chris. "What did you find down there?"

"Cobwebs mostly. The place looked like

Dracula's favorite dining room. Then I heard noises."

"What kind?"

Spice shuddered. "Horrible! I can hardly describe them. Sort of a gibbering. I couldn't tell whether it was animal or human."

"Couldn't you see where the noises were coming from?" Geronimo put in.

She shook her head. "I started searching, but it was slow going with just my small flashlight. There were huge wine casks and some old stone coffins with figures of the dear departed carved on top. Also some old medieval torture devices, like an Iron Maiden and a rack."

"Is that what made you scream?" Chris asked.

Spice looked at him scornfully. "I am not afraid of spooks, my dear Christopher. It just happens that a flock of ferocious-looking bats came swooping out of the darkness. One flew right at me! I had to fight it off!"

Spice shuddered again at the recollection. "It wasn't only the bats," she went on. "I heard steps coming through the darkness, so I decided it was high time to powder out of there."

Chris and Geronimo looked at each other with puzzled frowns. "What makes gibbering noises?" Chris said thoughtfully.

"Q does sometimes when he gets real peeved," said Geronimo, "but I don't suppose *he* was down

ere. Maybe it was the bats, although they just
queak, as far as I know."

"These were ghastly!" Spice's voice quivered.
The way they came swooping toward me!"

"You probably disturbed one of their nesting
laces when you were shining your flashlight
round," said Chris.

"Maybe." Spice sounded doubtful. "I know I
as worked up and all that, but somehow these
idn't seem like ordinary bats. Ugh! If I hadn't
vatted one with my shoe, he might have bit
e!"

"There's also the question of what Moutin was
ping down in the tunnel," Chris added.

"I think the main tunnel must lead to the cha-
au kitchens," said Geronimo. "I noticed other
rvants with trays coming and going between
ose hedges earlier in the evening."

Meanwhile, the count's fete was gradually
rawing to a close. As Chris related his adven-
re in the tower to Spice, a few of the guests
egan to leave. Presently the TEEN agents no-
ced Valaud wandering about the grounds as if
oking for his companion.

"Oh, oh! We'd better scram," said Chris. "If
arone comes staggering out of the bushes in his
nderwear, there's apt to be trouble."

Spice giggled nervously. "We might miss out
the high point of the party. But I suppose

you're right. Someone may call the gendarmes.

Chris got up from the garden bench. "Let blow before the excitement starts."

Spice excused herself to Madame Avril an the three hurried to the parking area withou bothering to take leave of their host. Chri opened the door of the Alfa-Romeo for Spic Suddenly he stiffened in alarm.

The bundle of wet clothes was gone!

15 · Orders in Code

"SOMEONE'S HEISTED MY wet clothes!" said Chris.

"Anything in the pockets?" Spice asked.

Chris shook his head. "That's not what's worrying me."

"What is?"

"Those clothes were a dead giveaway that I'm the phony African who dived off the tower."

"Oh dear!" Spice's emerald-green eyes widened anxiously. "How much can the thief deduce from that?"

"Plenty, if he knows anything about that X mark on the chart. All he has to do is put two and two together. This could finger me as the agent who came here to contact X."

The TEEN agents eyed one another uneasily.

"There's also the fifty G's," said Geronimo. "Or maybe I should say there *was*."

Spice gasped. "See if the money's still in the secret compartment!"

"Not now," Chris said. "Hop in. We'll stop along the road and check."

A moment later the car was speeding down the hillside driveway from the chateau.

"Anyone on our tail?" the Apache muttered.

Chris looked. "No sign, unless he's running without lights."

On the highway between Brécy and Madame Avril's Lycée, Chris pulled over among some trees. Geronimo flipped back the carpeting and pressed the release button. The panel covering the secret compartment slid open.

Spice let out a sigh of relief as she saw the zippered case lying safely inside.

"Let's make sure the wampum's still here," Geronimo said cautiously. He unzipped the leather case. Inside were the neat packs of currency. "Okay, we're financially solvent."

Chris grinned dryly. "Boy! Imagine explaining *that* to Q if we weren't."

"I hate to bring it up," said Spice, "but you still have the small problem of which X to contact."

"I know—and I hate to *have* you bring it up.

Let's sleep on it. Somehow I don't feel the old brain's ticking at peak efficiency just now."

When they dropped Spice at the Lycée, she hesitated before bidding the boys good night.

"Those stolen clothes worry me," she murmured. "So please! Don't take any chances!"

"We'll watch it," Chris promised. "Luckily Apaches sleep with one eye open."

As they drove off, Geronimo said, "You know, *choonday*, it might be smart for us not to bunk at the hotel tonight."

Chris shot a thoughtful glance at his partner. "You mean check out and find some place else?"

"Not even check out. If anyone comes looking for us there in the wee hours, we'll just give him a nice long wait."

"Hm! It's an idea—but we may have trouble finding other accommodations with the festival on."

"What about Dijon?" Geronimo suggested. "It's only a few miles away. A city that size would give us plenty of cover."

Chris nodded. "Sounds like a good bet."

The Alfa-Romeo skirted around Brécy and headed east. Half an hour later, the two youths were registering at a small hotel in the olden-time capital of the Dukes of Burgundy.

Next morning they breakfasted on eggs and sausages at a small café near the hotel.

"What's our next move, fearless leader?" said Geronimo.

Chris mulled over the situation as he sipped his coffee. "Ravatsky, Fernac, Moutin—as far as I can see, the odds are about equal on all three of them. Looks as if we'll have to play it by ear."

"A bit more specific, please."

"Well, suppose I try phoning each one, without giving my name. I drop a few hints and see how he reacts. Maybe their answers will give us a line on which one is the real X."

The Apache considered. "Okay. It's worth a try, but how'll you locate Fernac?"

"Don't know yet. He shouldn't be too hard to run down, though, if he's our man."

Chris decided to try Ravatsky first. From a telephone booth, he called the Agricultural Institute. Disguising his voice and speaking French, he asked for the chemist.

"I am sorry, but Monsieur Ravatsky is not here," said the switchboard operator. "He phoned to say that he would not be in today. We do little work here during the festival, you see."

"Could I reach him at his residence?" Chris inquired.

"I am afraid not, monsieur. He was leaving early for a weekend on the Côte d'Azur—in fact he phoned from somewhere on the road. But you could call him this evening at St. Tropez. He will be staying at the Hotel des Palmes."

"Merci." Hanging up, Chris reported the conversation.

"Something fishy there, eh?" said the Apache.

"How come he leaves town all of a sudden after wearing that X mark on his hand last night?"

"Just what I'm wondering," Chris responded. "Gerry, I have a hunch Ravatsky's our boy—and he may be expecting Omega to follow him!"

"Why so?"

"Look. If Ravatsky were an enemy agent, trying to cut in on Skykill, he wouldn't be leaving town. He'd want to stick around and find out what cooks. Right?"

"Sounds reasonable."

"But suppose he's the real X," Chris went on. "He might figure something went wrong last night, or maybe just that Omega was afraid to make contact with so many people around. Either way, Ravatsky decides he'd better clear out. If there's been a foul-up, he'll be safer away from Brécy. On the other hand, if Omega's just being cautious, this will give him a chance to make the contact in different surroundings."

"That adds up, all right," Geronimo said. "But what about Fernac and Moutin? Are you still going to call them, too?"

Chris shook his head. "One thing at a time. No sense stirring up the broth any more than we have to. Let's put the sleeve on Ravatsky first. If he doesn't produce, we'll try the other two."

"So we're off to St. Tropez on the Riviera?"

"Roger. Let's go back to Brécy, check out of the hotel there, and pass the word to Spice. Then we'll hit the road south."

At Brécy the desk clerk greeted the boys with a beaming smile. "Ah, *bon jour, messieurs!* You have a letter, Monsieur Cool. It just arrived *exprès* this morning from Paris."

He fumbled in a slot behind the counter, then handed over an envelope and their room key.

"*Merci,*" said Chris. "By the way, we'll be checking out shortly."

As they started up to their floor in the ancient, creaking elevator, Geronimo murmured, "Well, well—news from Uncle Phil, eh?"

"Let's hope it's nothing drastic," said Chris.

Once in their room, Chris slit open the envelope. He glanced at the letter inside—a chatty, hand-scrawled note about the latest doings of Uncle Phil and Aunt Maud—and tossed it in the wastebasket.

Geronimo, meanwhile, got the toilet kit from his suitcase, removed its contents, and began converting it into a small microfilm projector. The false-bottomed metal drinking cup unscrewed to provide a powerful set of lenses.

Chris located a small black dot on the envelope which looked like part of the typewritten address. He inserted it in the projector and

vitched on a tiny, high-intensity bulb. A white
illow slip served as the screen. Presently, as he
ljusted the lenses, the microdot message came
ito focus.

"Okay, break out the codebook, Injun."

Geronimo took a European travel guidebook
om their luggage and began checking out each
nit of the message. Translated, the message
ead:

COMPLETE PRESENT MISSION SOONEST. ORDERS
JUST RECEIVED FOR YOU BOTH TO REPORT VI-
ENNA APRIL 30.

"*Ai!*" Geronimo exclaimed. "Vienna's in Aus-
ia and April thirtieth is next Sunday, just two
ays away. Why the sudden switch?"

Chris frowned thoughtfully. "Must have some-
ning to do with that international conference.
he President's flying to Vienna that day. Re-
nember the clipping in Barone's pocket?"

"Yes, now that you mention it. But where do
e fit in? That doesn't give us much time to get
ifo on Skykill."

"We might swing it, if we barrel down to the
iviera pronto and Ravatsky comes through. We
ould probably hop an airline flight to Vienna
om Nice or Milan."

Chris glanced at his wrist watch and added,
I think we'd better call Uncle Phil first. If we

snap to it, we can catch him on the ten A.M
open-transmission schedule."

The boys checked out of the hotel hastily an
drove off. Once they were outside of Brécy
Geronimo pressed a button on the dashboard
causing a radio antenna to spear up from a rea
fender. Then he tuned in the short-wave tran
ceiver and scrambler, and quickly made contac
with Paris.

Chris picked up the mike. "Wunny Kingsto
to Phil."

"Phil here. Go ahead, please."

Chris gave the CIA station chief a rapid rur
down on their situation, then asked, "What abou
these orders to Vienna?"

"Summit Power Conference," Grubb replie
tersely. "All agents on the continent are bein
routed there to beef up security when the Pres
dent arrives. There's a special reason why Wash
ington wants you two on hand."

"Oh? What is that, sir?"

"You know what this conference is about?"

"It was called to discuss a ban on the H-bom
and all atomic weapons, wasn't it?"

"Right. Now then," Grubb went on, "if an
nation at the meeting has Skykill up i
sleeve, that'll give it a big trump card to ba
gain with. So it's important that you fill in th
President on anything—anything at all—tha

you've picked up on Skykill. The top scientific brains in our defense setup will be there to help analyze the information."

"Understood." Chris suppressed a faint feeling of butterflies in his stomach. "By the way, Alexandre Valaud was at the count's fete last night. A man with him, named Barone, was carrying Omega's letter-drop key. It might be worth while putting a tail on him."

The boys caught a faint, startled gasp over the radio speaker. "Apparently you haven't heard," Grubb said after a moment.

"Heard what?"

"Valaud and Barone crashed last night in Valaud's private plane."

It was Chris's turn to gasp. "Any survivors?"

"None. Better get a paper and read the story."

Chris U-turned the car and headed back into Brécy. At a café-*tabac* the boys found a morning edition of the Dijon *Les Dépêches*. It carried a full account of the crash.

Valaud's plane had taken off from Longvic airfield near Dijon at 2 A.M. Twenty minutes later it had crashed near Montbard en route to Paris. The wreckage was widely scattered as if the plane had come apart in mid-air. Just before the disaster the pilot had radioed frantically:

"Ice is forming all over the plane! It's fantastic! The ship is going out of control!"

Chris and Geronimo exchanged stunned glances.

"Sounds like another job by the Chiller," the Apache muttered.

"If it was, he has a long reach." Chris stared at his partner. "You realize what this means, Gerry? If the Chiller can knock a plane out of the air, the gimmick he's using may be Skykill itself!"

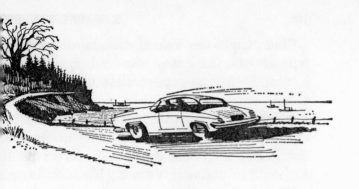

16 · Road Hazards

CHRIS'S THEORY SENT a tingle of excitement through the TEEN agents. Perhaps they had been closer to Skykill than they had realized.

Dangerously close. Anson had already been iced and Chris had had a hairbreadth escape. If the device worked with such terrible effect at long range, the Chiller might strike again, when least expected!

The boys were thoughtful as they got back into their car and drove out of Brécy.

"Well, one good thing," mused Geronimo. "At least we can be pretty sure the Reds don't have Skykill."

"Not if it was used against two of their own agents," Chris agreed.

"But why were Valaud and Barone rubbed out? Do you think they stumbled on something last night—maybe got too close to the Chiller's secret?"

Chris shrugged as they left the town behind and headed along the road leading to Madame Avril's Lycée. "Could be, but somehow I doubt it. Looks to me as if Valaud's big mistake was coming here at all. He was a known Red spy master and I have a strong hunch the Chiller doesn't like snoops."

At the Lycée, Spice was excused from her morning class long enough to say good-by to her two friends. The TEEN agents strolled about the school grounds as Chris briefed her.

"Too bad," Spice needled playfully. "I'll bet you hate the whole idea, having to chase way down to the Riviera with all those palm trees and nice white sandy beaches. And girls."

"Look! These aren't the Rites of Spring we're attending at Florida beaches," said Chris. "We're going down to check out one lead on Skykill, and it could be dangerous."

Spice's green eyes twinkled. "In that case, are you sure you won't need help?"

"Have bikini, will travel, I presume?" Chris grinned and shook his head. "Be a great idea if this were a surfing jaunt, but it isn't and you'd better stay put. For that matter it might be mart to stay close to the school. After all, you were seen with us last night."

"Remind me to be more careful about whom I date." Spice dimpled, then became serious. "Think you'll need me again on this assignment?"

"We may if Ravatsky's the wrong X. At least hang around till we find out. We'll get word to you from St. Tropez if we locate what we're after."

Spice exchanged a TEEN-agent grip with each of the boys and waved as they drove off.

"Not a bad little squaw," Geronimo said grudgingly.

"Don't tell me they come any greater at the Mescalero Agency."

"To each his own, *choonday*—to each his own." Geronimo gazed out the car window and began humming a plaintive Apache ballad.

The boys sped south through the beautiful farming country of the Saône River. By twelve-thirty they were lunching in the great textile city of Lyons. From there, they followed the wide concrete ribbon of Route Nationale 7 down the Rhône Valley.

The sun grew hotter and brighter. Silvery olive groves and windbreaks of tall, graceful cypress trees appeared along the way.

From Avignon, the ancient city of the Popes

with its beautiful twelfth-century bridge, the
route veered east through Aix-en-Provence, and
at last they reached the sea at Fréjus. Here
they turned down the coastal highway toward
St. Tropez.

The sky was a brilliant blue and the air full of
flowery scents. The road skirted a rocky massif
topped by forests of Aleppo pine, chestnut, and
cork oak. Much of the time they were in sight of
the Mediterranean, smooth and clear as a sap
phire. Settlements of villas dotted the shore.

Soon after six o'clock they rounded the Gulf of
St. Tropez and turned onto the pleasant wooded
peninsula where the resort town was situated.
Chris jammed on the brakes as a man darted out
onto the road, waving his arms.

"Must've had a breakdown," Chris said.

Off the highway stood a little Triumph convert
ible, mustard yellow, with its hood raised. Chris
pulled over behind it.

The man who had signaled for help walked up
to the driver's side of the Alfa-Romeo. He was a
short, thin fellow with a straw hat and steel
rimmed glasses which gave him the mild but busi
nesslike air of a bank clerk or bookkeeper.

"Car trouble?" Chris inquired.

The man's lips twisted into a toothy, ratlike
grin. From his coat pocket he pulled out an odd
shaped device with a tube at one end.

"Outside, messieurs!" he rasped.

"I beg your pardon?" Chris said with a look of polite surprise.

"Out of your car! *Vite!*" The man squeezed the device he was holding. A thin stream of liquid squirted through the open window, sending up a faint wisp of smoke as it seared a hole in the upholstery on Geronimo's side. "You saw what just happened? Acid, *mes amis!* It can burn holes in your faces as well as in leather. Now move— quickly!"

Chris and Geronimo looked at each other and shrugged. Chris reached out to open the door. His thumb pressed a hidden button. As the door swung open, there was a sudden hiss—a blunt missile shot out at blinding speed!

The missile caught the stranger square in the face, knocking him over like a bowling pin. He sprawled on his back in the roadway with blood oozing from his nose. Chris leaped out to snatch up the acid weapon. But there was no need for haste. The man had been knocked senseless by the hard wooden projectile.

Geronimo hurried around to his partner's side of the car. Chris recovered the missile and loaded it back into its socket. Then they dragged their unconscious foe off the road into the shelter of some trees and dense shrubbery.

"We could have warned him, but I don't suppose he would have listened," said Chris.

Geronimo gave a dry chuckle. "That's so true,

choonday. These gung-ho types, you can't te
them anything."

"Well, let's find out who he is." Chris friske
the man's pockets deftly but learned nothing
Geronimo, meanwhile, searched the Triump
convertible and likewise drew a blank.

"What'll we do?" the Apache asked.

Chris shrugged. "Disable his car and leav
him—"

He broke off as another car came whizzing to
ward them. The two boys walked hastily towar
the Alfa-Romeo and pretended to be studying :
road map until the car had zoomed past.

Chris accompanied his partner back into th
woods fringing the road. Both boys stopped short
The man was gone! He had evidently fle
through the underbrush.

"That way! He left a clear enough trail!" Chri
exclaimed.

The boys had covered only a few yards whe
Geronimo shouted, "There he goes!"

A figure had just darted from the brush. Th
man was doubling back to his parked car. Chri
and Geronimo sprinted after him. He slamme
the convertible's hood, leaped in, and gunned th
engine. The Triumph shot forward with a roa
forcing the TEEN agents to fling themselve
aside to keep from being run down.

The boys picked themselves up without a wor
and rushed to the Alfa-Romeo. Chris slid behin

the wheel and they took off with a squeal of rubber. In seconds, from a standing start, the car had
accelerated to 140 miles.

Ahead, the Triumph was straining to hold its
lead. The driver, instead of following the Gulf
road into St. Tropez, cut right onto the highway
that branched across the peninsula. He skirted
the hillside village of Gassin, perched among the
oak woods, and sped on over a steep rise.

Chris bore down grimly, nursing every ounce
of power from his engine. The chase made him
more and more determined to overtake their
quarry and wring the truth from him. If they
could discover and thwart the unknown enemy's
plans, it might spell the difference between suc-
cess or failure for their mission.

Bit by bit they were closing in. Ahead lay a
sharp turn in the hill road. The Triumph took it
flat-out, tires screeching as the convertible's rear
end slewed dangerously.

The mustard-yellow sports car was halfway
around the turn when its driver lost control. The
car swerved and slid, slewing almost ninety de-
grees. A front wheel jounced on the shoulder of
the road. The next instant the car went sailing
over the embankment!

17 · Mark of the Toad

TOPPLING END OVER end, the Triumph hurtled down the rocky hillside, its driver thrown out like a rag doll. A moment later the car crashed to a halt on a spur of rock.

Boom! Spilled gasoline exploded. A pillar of fire shot up from the wreck and the convertible became wrapped in a cocoon of flame.

Chris had brought his car to a screeching halt. The boys leaped out and stared down from the edge of the road. The driver lay twisted and still, far down the slope.

"At least he's clear of the fire," Chris muttered tensely after a moment.

"Should we go down after him?" Geronimo asked.

Chris shook his head. "We'd better get a doctor first. It might be fatal to move him. Besides, we can't risk getting mixed up with the police and held for questioning."

The boys returned to their car and sped on. Chris stopped at a roadside restaurant and gas station outside Croix-Valmer on the south shore of the peninsula. He called the local police from a phone booth and reported the accident. Then the TEEN agents headed back for St. Tropez.

It was not yet seven o'clock when the boys drove into St. Tropez. Once a mere fishing village and artist colony, the town had become the most popular resort on the Riviera. Though the season had not yet begun, the harbor was lively with people in gay-colored sun clothes, and boats of all sizes were moored at the quays.

Chris parked on the broad Quai de Suffren. Beyond the cafés and shops surrounding the harbor were tall houses of pink, cream, yellow, and lavender. The bronze statue of a French admiral looked out over the water.

"Stay here and keep your eyes open," Chris told Geronimo. "I'll go see about Ravatsky."

The Hotel des Palmes was only a short way from the waterfront. Like most other hotels in St. Tropez, it was a modest, informal establishment. Chris inquired at the desk for Ravatsky.

"Room 318, monsieur."

As the blond TEEN agent turned to go upstairs, the concierge called, "*Pardon,* but you will not find him in his room. I remember now that Monsieur Ravatsky went out—oh, about five o'clock, soon after he arrived. He asked me about renting a boat."

"Then perhaps I can find him somewhere around the harbor," said Chris.

"*Oui,* you can find most anyone there at this hour—or else bowling *pétanque* on the Place des Lices." The concierge chuckled amiably.

Chris returned to his partner. Geronimo, who had been scanning the harbor through binoculars, listened and gave his pal a crafty look.

"Maybe it's a lucky break, him not being in."

Chris said, "You suggesting we case his room?"

"Why not? There's a lot at stake here—possibly including our necks. Wouldn't hurt to take a peek at the guy's credentials."

Chris thought for a moment, then gave a nod. "Okay. But I doubt if we can sneak past the concierge. The lobby's too small."

Geronimo grinned. "So we'll try the windows."

At the rear of the hotel was a small garden shaded by palm trees. A short ironwork balcony extended across part of each floor. On each of these balconies a central door apparently gave access to an inside corridor.

"It's a cinch," said Geronimo. "You stay down below and keep watch for Ravatsky."

The pink stucco wall was overgrown with vines. Nimbly the Apache shinned up a tile drainpipe with catlike ease, clutching the woody vine for extra support. On the third floor he swung over to the balcony. Its latched door gave him only a moment's pause. Then he disappeared inside.

Chris strolled around to the front of the hotel. Twenty minutes later Geronimo joined him.

"Find anything?" Chris asked.

Geronimo held out a small cylinder bearing a signet design at one end and a plunger at the other. "This was in Ravatsky's suitcase."

The signet design had been incised in such a way that the raised ridges were razor-sharp. He pressed it against the whitish bark of a plane tree and pushed the plunger. When he pulled the device away, the tree bark bore the deep-cut outline of a toad! Brown fluid oozed in the cut.

Chris gave a whistle. "TOAD's trademark!"

"Right. What they stamp on the foreheads of all their victims. Cute little gimmick, eh? And the brown stuff is deadly venom."

A caterpillar had been crawling up the tree trunk. It paused to sample the brownish fluid. The boys saw the tiny creature suddenly stiffen, then drop limply to the ground.

"See what I mean?" said Geronimo.

Chris repressed a shudder. "The venom works

even better on people, from what I hear. Boy, if Ravatsky's a TOAD agent, I might've been walking right into a trap!"

"Too right. They might've carried you out feet first with a toad stamped on your forehead."

Chris rubbed his jaw worriedly. "It's still possible Ravatsky's the real X. He may be hoping to cash in on a private deal with Omega."

"If you ask me," Geronimo argued, "it's ten times more likely that Ravatsky's one of the phony X's. He was probably just trying to horn in on Omega's deal."

"Then why come down to St. Tropez?"

"Maybe to decoy us into following him."

"And we bit." Chris nodded thoughtfully. "If you're right, the guy in the Triumph may have been hired by Ravatsky to nab us."

"Looks to me as if we'd better clear out and head back to Brécy," said Geronimo.

"Guess that's the only way to play safe," Chris agreed. "We'll have to check out Moutin and Fernac before we decide which way to jump."

The air was still and clear with the last moments of daylight as the boys returned to the harbor. Masts of boats moored at the quays swayed lazily in the breeze. Beyond the breakwater, the blue gulf stretched away to the opposite coast and far to the northeast the distant ridges of the Alps were fading into darkness.

Geronimo took a last look through the binocu

rs. "Oh, oh! Here he comes!" the Apache murmured.

A lone sailboat was just gliding into harbor past the breakwater. Its single occupant was standing erect in the cockpit to haul down the sail. Chris took the glasses and focused on him.

Sure enough—Ravatsky. He was wearing denim pants and a striped fisherman's jersey.

Suddenly Chris's hand tightened on the binoculars. A look of terror had come over Ravatsky's face. He let the sail fall and began to shiver violently. Through the high-powered lenses Chris could see his lips and cheeks turning blue with cold. Scales of ice were forming on his skin.

With a scream that echoed across the harbor Ravatsky toppled headfirst into the water!

18 · A Risky Rendezvous

"THE CHILLER GOT him!" Chris exclaimed. Ra
vatsky's scream had drawn the attention of a fis
erman, who leaped in to rescue him. Seconds late
a motorboat sped out from the Quai Jean Jaurè
Two others quickly followed.

Presently the fisherman surfaced, one han
cupping Ravatsky's chin. The victim's face looke
purple and his eyes were closed.

"*Ai!*" Geronimo muttered. "Whoever did
must be somewhere close by!"

Chris nodded, feeling a chill of apprehension a
he gazed around the harbor. The quays wer
lined with spectators, many of whom had rushe
from the surrounding cafés and shops. Any one o
them might be the Chiller or his agent! Or ha

he Chiller aimed his device from one of the windows overlooking the harbor? He might even be aboard one of the boats.

"We'd better blow before he spots *us!*" Chris advised.

The boys hastily piled into their car and Chris began threading through the crowded area.

At Fréjus they regained Route Nationale 7. It was nearly eleven o'clock when they finally pulled into a dimly lighted motel near the great Rhône Valley dam of Donzère-Mondragon. Chris was careful to park out of sight of the highway.

Next morning, over croissants and coffee, Geronimo said, "We haven't much time left, *choon-day.*"

Chris sipped. "Today's our last chance to find out anything. We'll have to head for Paris tomorrow and hop a plane for Vienna."

Geronimo toyed with his obsidian knife. "You realize we may be taking a risk showing up in Brécy again, if the Chiller's got our number."

"So?"

"That town's not very big. Maybe we'd be smarter not to go barging in during the daylight hours when we can easily be spotted."

Chris frowned thoughtfully. "That's a good point, Gerry. If we're going to contact Fernac and Moutin, we can do it just as well after dark—and maybe a lot more safely."

For the rest of the trip north, the boys cruised

at moderate speed. They ate supper at a countr
inn and approached Brécy after sunset.

Before entering the town, they stopped a
Madame Avril's Lycée to see Spice. The mistres
told them she was not at the school.

"Mademoiselle Carter went out half an hou
ago. But she left this note for you, Monsieur Coo
in case you arrived while she was gone."

Chris thanked her and went back to the ca
with Geronimo. The message—in basic TEEN
code—was dashed off in green ink. Translated, i
read:

> *X phoned this evening—at least he claimed
> to be X. Wanted to see you. Urgent. Sounded
> scared. Since you weren't in town, asked me
> to meet him instead. Let's hope I'm not mak-
> ing a horrible mistake. Appointment is for
> 7:30, a hundred paces from road at Roc du
> Diable. Wish you were here!*

Chris glanced tensely at Geronimo. "What d
you make of it?"

The Apache shrugged. "Even money. Could b
on the level or it could be a trick."

From having scouted the area on the afternoo
before the count's fete, both boys knew the loca
tion of Roc du Diable—a huge rock formation o
the road leading from town to the chateau.

Chris's wrist watch showed 7:42. He twirle
the stem and tugged it twice. The boys sat in th

ar, waiting, but Spice's voice did not answer.
Chris buzzed again. Still no response.

"I think we'd better go look for her—pronto!"
aid Geronimo.

"So do I. But not together."

"Why not?"

"No sense scaring off our pigeon if he's the real
K," said Chris. "Remember, Spice said he
ounded frightened. Let's drive past Roc du Di-
ble and I'll hop out. You keep going."

"Where to?"

"The nearest phone booth. This will give us a
chance to check on Fernac and Moutin. Try call-
ng both of them—Moutin at the chateau and Fer-
ac at the hotel. If he's not registered there, try
he other hostelries around Brécy."

"And what do I say when they come on the
ine?" Geronimo inquired.

"Nothing. Just hang up. If one of them isn't
vailable, we can probably assume he's the one
vho's meeting Spice."

"What about you?"

"I'll buzz you as soon as I find out what's what,"
Chris promised. "If you don't hear from me in
ialf an hour, notify Uncle Phil on the radio and
tart looking for us."

Geronimo nodded. He took the wheel and they
lrove away from the school toward Brécy. Skirt-
ng the edge of town, the red sports car turned
•nto the road leading to the chateau.

Presently their headlights picked out a tower
ing mass of granite rock. All around it was a dens
stand of pine, oak, and chestnut.

Chris had already taken the zipper case fror
the secret compartment. Inside were five packs c
currency. He tucked one into the pocket of hi
sports coat and returned the case to its hidin
place. Then, as Geronimo braked to a halt, h
jumped out and slammed the door.

"Okay. Take it away, Redskin."

"Watch yourself, *choonday*."

Chris walked around the clump of rock an
made his way into the woods. The moon was ou
and enough of a glow filtered through the trees t
guide him. Nevertheless, the night stillness an
the deep shadows made the atmosphere uncom
fortably spooky. It was easy to imagine an enem
lurking in the darkness.

Chris started as an owl hooted somewhere i
the arching branches. There was another noise
too. It seemed to be a humming sound comin
from somewhere below, almost as if it were risin
up from the forest floor.

He stopped, straining his ears, but now h
could hear nothing. A hundred paces brought hir
to a small clearing. Chris froze as a light flashed i
his face, then went out again.

"Ah . . . Monsieur Cool!" A figure was stand
ing in the clearing.

Chris switched on his own flashlight lon

enough to make out the speaker. It was the servant Moutin. His face glistened palely in the yellow glow. He seemed startled and nervous.

"You weren't expecting me?" Chris asked in a
hard, suspicious voice.

"*Mais non!* It is true I wished to see you, but
I—I thought your friend, Mademoiselle Carter,
was to come."

"So did I. Hasn't she been here?"

Moutin shook his head. "I have been waiting
for the past half hour."

Chris felt a pang of alarm. Had something happened to Spice? Then another question occurred
to him. "How did you know I was your contact?"
he asked Moutin.

"By the Omega symbol, of course."

"What Omega symbol?"

"Marked in crayon on your car window, the
night of the fete." Moutin's voice became suddenly anxious. "You put it there to identify yourself, did you not, after you saw the X on my hand?
I assume you thought that way was safer than
approaching me in public. I rubbed it off at once,
naturally."

Chris frowned. He had not crayoned the
Omega symbol on the Alfa-Romeo. But it was
possible that the Chiller's agents might have done
so after taking the wet clothes from his car.

"All right. Go on. You saw an Omega symbol on
my car. Then what?"

Moutin shrugged. "It was not difficult to find out your names from the guest list. But to be safe, I waited all yesterday, hoping you would make the first move. When you did not contact me, I called the hotel in Brécy. They said you had checked out. So I called Mademoiselle Carter at the Lycée."

Chris hesitated. Could he trust Moutin? There was no way to back out now, having once revealed himself.

"P-p-please, monsieur! Let us not stand around talking!" the servant begged. "Even the forest may have ears. Are you prepared to go through with the deal or not?"

"That depends on what you have to offer."

Moutin fidgeted nervously. "Have you any notion of what Skykill is, monsieur?"

"At a guess, some sort of long-range chilling device."

"Ah, quite correct. It works by a microwave action and can suck the heat out of any object— potentially at ranges up to several hundred miles. The effect is deadly against planes and ICBM missiles—even spacecraft, once they have entered the earth's atmosphere. The sudden chill causes structural failure."

"As happened with Valaud's plane the other night?"

Moutin nodded. "There is also a miniaturized version designed as an antipersonnel weapon."

"Who developed Skykill?"

"The basic idea was conceived by a genius—perhaps a madman—who calls himself *Le Glacier*. But the actual prototypes were built by a staff of scientists in a secret underground laboratory not far from where we are standing."

"I'm expecting a lot more than this for fifty thousand," the TEEN agent said.

"You shall have it, monsieur. I am prepared to take you to the laboratory itself."

Chris took out the bundle of bills. "There's the first installment. You'll get the rest when I've seen this laboratory with my own eyes."

Moutin examined the bills by the glow of his flashlight and stuffed them inside his coat. *"Eh bien.* At this moment no one is there and you will be able to take as many notes and photographs as you like. But we must go quickly, or the chance will be lost."

Chris's pulse began to race. His tiny f 1.5 buttonhole camera was loaded with film. "Okay. First let me call my partner."

He started to twirl the stem of his wrist watch. Moutin grabbed his arm. *"Non,* monsieur! If that is a radio, do not use it!"

"Why not?"

"There is an omni-frequency monitor near here. Your signal would touch off an instant alarm."

Chris frowned suspiciously, then shrugged "All right. Let's go."

"Only a few steps, monsieur." Moutin guide the TEEN agent toward the huge, sawed-o stump of an ancient oak tree, about two feet high "We must stand on this stump," the servant ex plained.

Puzzled, Chris complied. Moutin stepped u on the stump beside him, then took a small devic out of his pocket and pressed a button on it.

With a faint hum the entire oak stump began t sink down beneath the forest floor! It was th camouflaged elevator that had made the hum ming sound earlier!

"This is a secret entrance for the staff scientist so they will not attract attention by their coming and goings," said Moutin.

The elevator descended into a dimly lighted metal-walled tunnel. As they stepped off, th stump rose back into place.

"Straight ahead, monsieur."

The tunnel opened into a cement-floored cham ber. Chris's eyes roved around, taking in a power ful motor generator, a huge air-conditioning unit a control panel . . .

Suddenly the lights went out!

Chris tensed alertly in the pitch darkness. Hi ears picked up faint noises—the scuffing of fee across the cement. He reached out, gropin blindly, but his fingers met only empty air.

Cautiously Chris took out his flashlight and switched it on.

Moutin was gone!

As a weird, maniacal laugh echoed through the chamber, there was a sudden flapping of wings.

Chris pointed his flashlight toward the sound. A horde of ferocious-looking bats was zooming straight toward him!

19 · Air Force One

CHRIS'S SCALP CONTRACTED in a thrill of horror.
He had blundered into a trap! The TEEN agent
flung up his arms to beat off the repulsive creatures.

The next instant a light flared on again above
the tunnel entrance. Chris gave a shudder of relief as the bats rose all around him, soaring up to
the ceiling of the chamber. Clinging to the rough
limestone with their claws, they peered down at
him with impudent little snouty faces.

Chris turned to flee back into the tunnel,
though the single light left the far walls of the
chamber shrouded in darkness.

"Do not move, Monsieur Cool!" The shrill,
high-pitched voice seemed to come from every-

where and nowhere. "The bats ceased attacking
you in response to an ultrasonic whistle above the
range of human hearing. But at the first move to
escape they will go for you again! Their bite is
extremely virulent and results in permanent brain
damage—if you survive at all."

Again came the weird laugh—almost a giggle.
Chris realized it must be issuing from stereo-
phonic speakers installed about the chamber.

Should he risk a sudden dash? Chris tensed and
darted toward the tunnel entrance. At once the
bats dived like ghastly miniature kamikazes!

"Stop!"

Chris froze motionless and the bats soared upward again, back to their ceiling roost.

"Perhaps you thought I was bluffing, monsieur.
Now you know better. One more attempt to escape and I shall abandon you to your fate!"

There was something vaguely familiar about
the voice, yet Chris could not place it.

"All right, so I'm your prisoner. Now what?"

"You will learn that in due course."

Moutin emerged from the tunnel, armed and
smiling nastily. He switched on his flashlight,
which revealed another exit.

"That way, monsieur! Hands on your head!"

As they moved across the chamber, the bats
fluttered along watchfully. Chris strode through
an exit into another tunnel, convoyed by the
swarm of winged creatures.

Finally he discerned an opening ahead. It led
into a dank, stone-floored cellar festooned with
cobwebs. Somewhere ahead, a strange babble of
voices broke out.

Or were they voices? The sounds were a bestial
gibbering—the same noises Spice had heard
Chris's blood ran cold as they drew nearer. The
sounds were coming from a grating in the floor.

"Halt, monsieur!"

Moutin aimed the flashlight's beam through the
grate. Below lay an underground dungeon, evidently an oubliette which opened only at the top
Chris gasped. The dungeon was crowded with
half a dozen prisoners—wild-eyed, filthy
bearded. They stared up, jabbering and slavering

Moutin chuckled. "They are all victims of bat
bites—victims who were lucky enough to survive."

He conducted Chris across the cellar to another
grating and ordered him to lean against the wall
while being frisked. The bats continued to circle
and flutter above their heads.

Moutin took Chris's wallet, anesthetic pen,
camera, and other items of TEEN-agent equipment. He put a pack of chewing gum back in
Chris's pocket with a sneering laugh. "Keep this
It may help to stave your hunger. You will not
find our prison fare very appetizing."

After making Chris hand over his wrist watch
Moutin unlocked and opened the grating and or-

dered him to descend a short, steep flight of stone steps into the oubliette. Then he lowered the grate into place and locked it.

"I will leave the light on, so you will know bats are on guard." Chuckling, Moutin added, "But there is no danger of your breaking out!"

His face withdrew from view, and Chris heard his steps fading off across the stone floor.

"Nice going, Cool old boy," Chris thought bitterly. He had really walked into this one!

It was clear enough now what had happened. Spice must have been taken prisoner just before he arrived, and Moutin had resurfaced to make sure she had not been tailed to the rendezvous.

A faint tapping sound drew Chris's attention to the wall of the dungeon. Two long taps. A short tap. Another long tap.

International Morse code! Chris spelled out the letters as the tapping continued. The sender was asking in French: *Who are you?*

Chris looked around hastily for something to reply with. Among the filthy straw on the floor lay a few crumbled pieces of rock. Chris snatched up the biggest and pounded out:

American. Chris Cool. Who are you?

The reply was: *Fernac. Deuxième Bureau.*

So the "journalist" was actually a French secret service agent! And now he, too, was a prisoner of the Chiller!

As the code conversation went on, Chris

learned why Fernac had been sent to Brécy. More
than a week earlier, the Paris police had fished a
woman named Odette Cassis out of the Seine. She
was half-drowned and mentally deranged. But on
the following Monday night she had recovered
long enough to babble a strange story. A secret
agent named Omega was going to Chateau Brécy
to pick up information on Skykill from someone
with an invisible X mark on his left hand.

The Deuxième Bureau had been alerted and
next day the jewelry shop had been searched.
Omega's letter-drop box had already been looted.
The circumstances, however, bore out Odette's
story well enough so that Fernac had been sent to
the fete at Brécy to pose as X in the hope of
intercepting Omega and learning more.

Apparently *Le Glacier's* men had recognized
him as a French agent and he had been kidnapped from his hotel room that same night.

Chris gave a brief account of his own mission.

It was clear now that Odette must have been
the woman who had acted as go-between on X's
deal with Omega. Probably she was also the one
who had betrayed the deal to the Chiller.

The slow, tedious code tapping had gone on for
more than an hour. At last they stopped sending.

How to escape? Chris turned the problem over
and over in his mind. He had one secret weapon
still left at his disposal. He might use it to break

out. But the risk would be deadly dangerous in the confined space of his cell.

"Even if I lived to get out," Chris thought grimly, "there'd still be the bats."

The bats! Chris's heart leaped as an idea occurred to him. It was no guarantee of escape, but it might offer a fighting chance later!

He mounted the stone steps. Through the grating he could see the swarm of deadly bats clinging to the vaulted cellar ceiling. Chris stuck a hand through the bars and waggled it back and forth. Instantly the bats stirred into action, zooming down toward the living target!

Chris pulled back his hand just in time to keep from being bitten. Grinning with satisfaction, he took the pack of chewing gum out of his pocket. There were five sticks. Four contained various chemicals. The fifth contained a tiny microcircuit device in a flat sheath of plastic film.

Chris unwrapped the sticks, one by one, and popped them into his mouth. Mingled with his saliva, the chemical components began to react and produce a new, potent substance.

While he chewed, Chris took off his coat and ripped out the lining. He wrapped the material round his hand and reached out through the grate. The bats swooped down fiercely. Chris grabbed one and pulled it, squeaking, through the bars. By now the gum was wadded into a sticky ball. Chris plastered it firmly to the creature's furry back. Then he shoved the bat out through the bars and released it.

Nothing to do now but wait. Hours dragged by.

He was wakened by the clanking sound of the grate being opened. Moutin's face leered down.

"Up you come, Monsieur Cool! Quickly now!" He chuckled. "We must not keep *Le Glacier* waiting!"

Le Glacier! So at last Chris was to meet the deadly Chiller, face to face!

Nearby, another guard was rousting out Fernac. The French agent emerged, haggard and unshaven. The bats had fluttered down from their roost and were circling watchfully.

The two prisoners were conducted back to the generator chamber, then through another tunnel into a huge, brightly lighted laboratory workshop. The room was crammed with electronic gear, machine tools, and scientific equipment. A dozen men in white smocks, evidently engineers and technicians, were busily at work

At one end of the room was a broad desk workbench and a large control panel studded with monitor screens, dials, knobs, and switches. Beside it stood a massive, curious-looking console, apparently some sort of electronic unit.

Chris's eyes came to rest on three figures near the console. One was the Count de Brécy, dapper as ever. The others were Spice Carter and a guard on watch behind her.

A group of bats was roosting upside down on the ceiling above the trio. The swarm which had accompanied Chris and Fernac joined them.

Chris winked at Spice and she grinned back.

"Gee whillikers! We do seem to have got ourselves into a frightful mess, don't we?"

"Have no fear—Cool is here," Chris responded.

The count burst into a high-pitched giggle. "Admirable! Both in high spirits, I see. You will forgive these nasty bats, I hope. They are ferocious and act as watchdogs to attack any intruder unless restrained by a blast from one of these ultrasonic whistles."

The count picked up a metal cylinder from his desk. "My associates and I are also sprayed with a special scent, repugnant to the bats, which keeps them from attacking *us*."

"You, I take it," said Chris, "are *Le Glacier?*"

The count bowed mockingly. "I acquired that name in the early days of my experimenting. It was when I tested the first crude model of my invention on sample victims from the French underworld, as well as several unfortunate foreign agents."

The count tittered as if at an amusing joke. "Now you see before you the final, formidable model of *Ciel Assassin*—or Skykill if you wish."

He gestured to the console, then pressed a button. A steel panel in the wall slid aside to reveal a
periscopic view port. Through it, Chris and Spice
could see a hill across the river, topped by a lone
slender cypress tree. "That tree contains the
radiating antenna. Very soon you will see it in
action."

"This isn't your only model of Skykill, is it?"
Chris inquired.

"No indeed, monsieur." The count chuckled.
"Two exquisitely miniaturized portable models
were developed at great trouble and expense.
One was smuggled into your own country and
later destroyed over there to avoid any risk of
discovery. The other was used against you up on
the chateau tower. That one was later taken to St.
Tropez to deal with Ravatsky, as well as you and
your partner. That is, if my agent in the Triumph
had succeeded in kidnapping you on the road."

"You're undoubtedly a genius in your own
peculiar way," said Chris. "But why all the trouble to develop this mad-scientist gadget?"

The count's face darkened. "I am not a mad
scientist, my young friend. Someday I shall rule
France! To achieve that, one needs a powerful
organization—and TOAD has promised to place
all its resources at my disposal in exchange for the
use of Skykill."

Suddenly a number of pieces of the jigsaw fell

into place in Chris's mind. "So the Chiller and TOAD have been working together all along?"

"Exactly. Today's demonstration is a small job which I am carrying out for TOAD." The count's lips twisted into a cunning smile. "Maybe you would like to hear the whole story."

Chris shrugged. "Why not?"

"To begin with, I needed a staff of expert scientists. So I endowed an 'Agricultural Institute' as a cover for their presence in Brécy. One of those scientists was Ravatsky. But he became greedy and attempted to sell information on Skykill to a certain agent known as Omega."

"Then Ravatsky was the real X?"

"*Oui*. Unluckily for him, he used a friend named Odette Cassis to make the arrangements. But Odette was also greedy and she double-crossed Omega by selling out to TOAD."

Chris said, "And after TOAD found out all it wanted, it disposed of her?"

"Quite right—by injecting her with a mind-scrambling drug and dumping her into the Seine. First, of course, they kidnapped the jewelry-shop owner to check on her story and to squeeze out of him the real identity of Omega."

"And once you learned Omega was Anson, your agents proceeded to hunt him down?"

"Not mine—TOAD's. But of course we were working together."

"One was a frog-faced character?"

"*Oui*. He and two others trailed Anson to America and eliminated him." The count chuckled. "The job was not done as thoroughly as one might wish because you and your friend interrupted. Only Frogface returned. He had seen you at the amusement park and again on the plane coming to France. Once back in Paris, he tried to dispose of Brigitte Dubois and the painter Triquet, in case they had learned anything."

"But his ice cube trick didn't work."

"Alas, *non*—nor apparently did his attempt to ambush you on the Eiffel Tower."

This time it was Chris's turn to grin.

"Frogface made another blunder," the count went on. "He failed to find out your name and your partner's name, nor had he bothered to transmit your descriptions, since he expected to kill you in Paris. Thus we were left not knowing who might try to follow up Omega's lead."

"That's why you didn't rub out Ravatsky right away?" Chris inquired.

"*Oui*. In case of emergency, we had planned all along to save him as bait for a trap. At the fete Ravatsky was watched closely. Moutin, who is TOAD's liaison here, also wore an X on his hand in the hope that the American agent might contact him by mistake. But you were too cautious. However, we had prepared an alternate plan—a

X mark on the chateau diagram—to lure you up to the tower. This trap you fell into! But again you escaped."

"Not too well," Chris said grimly. "You knew I'd got soaked from diving into the river so you sent your men out to look for some telltale wet clothes, which they found in my Alfa-Romeo."

The count nodded. "So now that we had identified you, it remained only to eliminate you. You and your partner were to be iced in your hotel room that night, but you were too wary to sleep there."

"In the meantime," said Chris, "Ravatsky decided to go down to St. Tropez and give me a chance to contact him there."

"Precisely. This suited us very well, since we could now eliminate Ravatsky, you, and your partner at a safe distance from Brécy. But you two escaped from our road trap. Then a TOAD device was planted in Ravatsky's luggage to mislead you into thinking he was not the real X. This would insure that you came back to Brécy, where we could finish you once and for all."

"By the way," said Chris, "just how did your agent, or agents, manage to ice Ravatsky at St. Tropez harbor without anyone noticing?"

The count smiled and took from his desk what looked like a small hand movie camera. "Not very deadly in appearance, eh? Yet this is the portable

model of Skykill. The man who used it on Ravatsky seemed only to be photographing a boat coming into the harbor."

De Brécy placed it on top of the large console
model. "There you see them, my friend—the
small-scale and full-scale fruits of my genius!"

"*Monsieur le Comte!*"

Chris glanced around at the man who had spoken. He was wearing headphones and was seated
before a rack of electronic gear on which a red
light was now flashing. Beside him, another
operator was seated at a large digital computer.

"You have news, Jacques?" the count inquired.

"*Oui!* Air Force One passed the Paris check-
point seven minutes ago. It was positively identified by the radio transmissions between its pilot
and Paris Air Traffic Control. Our radar has now
locked on. You can see the blip on your monitor
screen if you wish."

Chris and Spice exchanged stunned glances.
*Air Force One was the personal plane of the
President of the United States!*

The count switched on his radarscope, then
smiled grimly. "I can see that you have already
guessed, *mes enfants*. The President's plane is
now heading this way, bearing him and his top
advisers to the Summit Power Conference in
Vienna. . . . In a few moments they will pass
within range of Skykill!"

20 · Bat Bomb

A SMALL BLIP could be seen moving slowly toward the center of the count's radarscope, painted by the revolving finger of light that swept around the screen.

The count stepped to his Skykill console and switched on power to the circuitry. After adjusting various knobs and dials, he pointed to the periscope window. "The weapon is now being aimed."

The two TEEN agents saw the tall tip of the cypress tree bend slightly to westward. Spice gave Chris a frantic look. In moments the wings and fuselage of Air Force One would begin to ice over. Soon, as its structural members weakened and gave way from the brittle chilling effect of Skykill, the plane would be torn apart in mid-air. The President and America's key defense experts would crash to destruction!

Noticing Spice's look, the guard clamped a warning hand on her shoulder. "Do not try anything foolish, mademoiselle!" he snarled.

Chris took a deep breath. It was now or never! With a sudden lunge, he darted across the floor toward Skykill.

"Down, Spice!" Chris yelled.

The deadly bats were already swooping to attack. The count, Moutin, and two guards who had moved to intercept Chris now drew back hastily to let the bats zoom in on their victim.

Chris dived face down on the floor behind the console. For the moment it shielded him from the bats. In the same instant his finger flicked the prong of his belt buckle.

This prong was a switch to the radio transmitter inside his belt. Instantly the transmitter flashed a triggering signal to the microcircuit detonator in the wad of explosive gum plastered on the bat's back.

Ka-boom!

There was a blinding flash and a stunning concussion. Fragments of the shredded bats and electronic debris flew through the air.

It was several moments before Chris recovered his wits. His head was still ringing from the blast.

The explosive gum, designed for blowing enemy safes and cell doors, rather than demolition work, had served his purpose! Both models of Skykill had been blown to smithereens!

Chris looked around hastily, while struggling to his feet. Fernac had followed the TEEN agents' lead and flung himself face down. Both he and Spice appeared unhurt and were getting up. The count, Moutin, and the two guards, however, had caught the full shock wave from the blast as well as the shrapnel effect of the flying fragments. All lay motionless.

The count's other men—the white-smocked technicians—were still on their feet. They stared in dismay at the unexpected scene.

"Let's go!" Chris seized Spice's arm. Fernac followed as the TEEN agents dashed for the tunnel.

But several of the count's men were racing to cut off their escape. The others were closing in behind them. Everyone came together in a wild, colliding melee!

Spice was nearly as good at judo and karate as Chris. She sent one man crashing to the floor with a hand-sword chop and kicked another neatly in the chin. Chris flung his nearest assailant over his shoulder, then butted his head into the solar plexus of the next. Fernac, meanwhile, was fighting with calm, deadly skill.

But the close quarters and weight of numbers were against the three secret agents. They were in danger of being overwhelmed by the sheer pile-up.

Suddenly a bloodcurdling war whoop echoed through the tunnel. "*Les Apaches!*" someone screamed. "*Sauve qui peut!*"

Chris recognized the yell as Geronimo's voice. But the effect on the count's men was demoralizing. They wavered and looked around for the nearest escape route. The next moment Geronimo was among them like a wolf in a sheepfold. Heads crashed together and teeth splintered.

Ten minutes later the cowed remnants of the count's men who were still on their feet had been lined up facing the wall. The secret agents held them covered with weapons taken from Moutin and the guards.

"Oh, good grief! I may faint!" gasped Spice in a sudden girlish reaction.

Geronimo chuckled. "This I want to see."

"By the way, Gerry, just how did you manage to get here?" Chris asked.

"It was really nothing, old chap," said the Apache. "I spent half the night trying to figure why you left no trail out of the clearing. Then I hid in the woods, in case the Chiller and his goons might be looking for me. This morning I got the sudden idea of exploring the mysterious, bat-haunted cellar that Spice discovered the night of the fete. Eventually I found the tunnel that led here."

"All three of you deserve the Legion of Honor!" Fernac declared.

"Is anybody—well—you know—dead?" Spice asked falteringly, not wanting to look around.

"I believe they all will recover from their injuries," the French secret agent replied. "Possibly even the Count de Brécy . . . although I fear the outlook for his health may not be too good when French justice comes to deal with him."

Twenty-four hours later the three TEEN agents were standing at attention in the presidential suite in Vienna.

"I understand, then, that Skykill is completely destroyed?" the Chief Executive asked.

"Yes, Mr. President," Chris replied. "The Count de Brécy was the only person who knew the overall assembly and carried the whole design in his head. He refused to let the doctors operate to save him."

"Any danger that the Reds acquired anything?"

"No, sir."

Chris explained that coded reports from Vaaud's network had been found in the Red spymaster's office. They showed how his agents had discovered the Chiller was hunting down Anson. From this, Valaud guessed that Anson must have stumbled on some important secret.

A watch had been kept on Anson's fiancée, and

later Barone had succeeded in stealing the Omega key from Triquet's studio. He had recognized it as a key to the letter-drop setup at Hoche's jewelry shop and had gone there immediately to raid Omega's box.

In the box was a follow-up note—unsigned, but no doubt from Ravatsky—asking for confirmation of the meeting at the count's fete. This clue had brought Valaud and Barone to Brécy. The count had guessed their purpose and decided to crack up their plane with Skykill.

"Brigitte Dubois and Triquet," Chris added, "have been located and are now safely back in Paris."

The President smiled approvingly and shook hands, one by one, with Chris, Spice, and Geronimo. "You have discharged your mission with skill and valor," he said, "and rendered a great service to the whole free world. Your chief has recommended all of you for the highest TEEN-agent award. In the meantime, how about a week's vacation in Paris as guests of the State Department before returning to your studies?"

He flushed and looked rather startled as Spice flung her arms around his neck and planted a loud smack on his cheek.

"Oh, Mr. President!" Spice exclaimed. "What a smashing idea!"

GERONIMO
JOHNSON